I0542472

A PARADISE
TO DIE FOR

David James Dixon

Grosvenor House
Publishing Limited

The right of David James Dixon to be identified as the author of this
work has been asserted in accordance with Section 78
of the Copyright, Designs and Patents Act 1988

The book cover is copyright to David James Dixon

This book is published by
Grosvenor House Publishing Ltd
Link House
140 The Broadway, Tolworth, Surrey, KT6 7HT.
www.grosvenorhousepublishing.co.uk

This book is a work of fiction. Any resemblance to
people or events, past or present, is purely coincidental.

A CIP record for this book
is available from the British Library

ISBN 978-1-83975-135-6

FOR ROSANNA

with love and thanks for all her support and encouragement

Content

✿

Athens

Aegina

Mykonos

Naxos

Paros

Antiparos

Irakleia

Koufonisia

Amorgos

Ios

Santorini

Anafi

Aegean Sea

☙

CHAPTER ONE

Friday, 31st May 2019

Piraeus

This was the best time to visit the Greek Islands. The weather was warm, the ferries were not crowded and it was easy to pick up a good deal at a hotel anywhere.

The tourist season had not officially kicked in yet, it was in start up mode. Lots of young Greeks were heading to the Islands to take up summer jobs. Hotels were readying themselves for the influx and madness that came in July and August, conducting minor repairs and giving a fresh lick of paint everywhere.

The end of May and early June was the favoured time for visitors that referred to themselves as genuine travellers, rather than tourists.

Jordan was a freelance photographer and loved the freedom that his chosen profession afforded him. He made a good living, picking up work in his home town of Canterbury, and from opportunist assignments in many of the Mediterranean locations that he visited during May through to October. This year, he had begun his travels in Greece in the last week of May.

He lay on the single bed in the budget accommodation on Praxitelous Street, located in a busy shopping district of Piraeus, the main seaport of Athens. He stared up at the ceiling and listened to the sound of a couple enjoying an early morning hump in the room above.

A few minutes earlier he had been in a deep sleep having a strange dream. He could not get the dream out of his mind, it was so vivid, and it disturbed him. He closed his eyes and tried to get back to sleep, maybe he could conjure up part two of the dream? After a few seconds he sat up in bed, laughing at himself for his silly thought.

He lay awake and returned to the imagery of the dream. The girl approached him and stared into his eyes. She slowly removed a scarf from around her neck and revealed a fresh scar. It was L-shaped and it cut across her windpipe. He asked her, 'Who hurt you sweetheart?' She did not reply, she just touched him on his cheek as she cried silently. That dream had kept repeating, over and over, like a needle sticking on a record player.

The girl in his dream was the waitress he had seen five days ago in a small family owned restaurant on Koufonisia. He had been drawn to her through her natural beauty as he watched her working the tables. They had only exchanged a few words, but he was sure there was a connection between them, not a spark, just a feeling of familiarity.

—⁓—

The coffee shops were cranking up for a busy day of service in Pasalimani. Its dual marinas offered the solo traveller a great people watching experience and the

2

opportunity to enjoy the vibe of outdoor life, without feeling too alone.

As Jordan downed his Greek coffee and stared at the sludgy remnants in the bottom of the small cup, the image of the girl returned. The weird mind pop was getting to him. He had already checked out of the hotel and should have been enjoying the morning air and working out his plan to travel up to the Sporades Islands. But this dammed recurring image was messing with his mind. He gave into it and decided to travel south instead, Skopilos would have to wait for now. Thanks to the copulating couple in the room above, he would have time to catch one of the early ferry sailings and return to Koufonisia by mid afternoon. He left four Euros on top of his receipt, waved over to the waiter and shouted, 'Efharisto.' Then he pulled his backpack over his shoulder and headed down to the main ferry terminal.

———

Being in the port of Piraeus at 7am always gave him a buzz. Most of the ferries serving the Islands were still berthed and preparing to sail. Scores of yellow taxis were arriving and dropping off couples, families and folks just like himself. All of the arriving hordes shared the same eagerness to board the ships and make the journey to somewhere special, somewhere they connected with or somewhere new that they wanted to explore.

He stepped onboard one of the large blue ships and made his way up through the decks to the external sitting area. This was a ferry journey he had done many times, but he never tired of it. He would pick the same spot to sit every time, the second deck level at the rear of the ship, and he would choose a table one row in from the stern of the ship, always with a view of the large Greek flag proudly hanging from its mast and flapping in the wind. From this position he could watch as the ferry sailed away from the mainland and slowly headed south, allowing the islands to present themselves one by one until he finally reached his destination.

―――

Koufonisia

The ferry was skilfully manoeuvred to line up with the small pier, churning up the dazzling clear turquoise waters as it came to rest. Within seconds of the ramp touching the pier, passengers and cars were spilling out onto the beautiful island of Koufonisia.

Jordan waited for the crowds to disperse before disembarking. He followed the road around to the small beach adjacent to the port and turned left to head up to the restaurant and the girl that had compelled him to return.

As he approached the steps leading up to the rooftop dining area, he felt a pang of nerves in his stomach. The dining area was deserted. He took a seat at a table overlooking the narrow main road that wound up through the Chora. He could hear someone in the kitchen area downstairs, but they must not have noticed him entering the restaurant. He waited a few more minutes and, just as he was about to seek assistance, he felt the presence of someone standing next to him. It was a waitress, but not the one in his dream.

The young lady smiled and used the Greek word for hello, 'Yasas,' and waited for him to place an order.

Jordan felt disappointed that it was not his waitress, 'Could I have a beer please, a large Mythos.' As she scribbled the order on her pad, he asked her, 'Where is the other waitress that works here? The tall girl with the long dark hair?'

She looked for confirmation from him as she suggested, 'Katerina?'

'Yes, I think that's her, she was working here about five days ago.'

'Mmm, no one has seen her for a few days. I am her replacement until she returns.'

Slightly concerned Jordan asked. 'Is she still on Koufonisia?'

'We don't think so. She has a flat above the bakery, we've called around there several times but there is no reply when we knock. Looks like her things are still in the room though.' She shrugged her shoulders and continued. 'Maybe she has gone back to Athens. It happens, summer girls often get homesick. We have left a couple of messages on her phone but she has not responded. Are you a friend of hers?'

'Kind of.' Jordan replied.

As Jordan finished his beer and left the restaurant, he was beginning to feel a little foolish. He had travelled all the way back to the island and for what? A strange recurring dream? Now it was beginning to look like the girl had simply headed off to visit her family in Athens.

The beer had stirred his appetite, it was time to eat. He hadn't had anything since breakfast in Pasalimani. The smell of the gyros coming from a Tavern just down the hill was adding to his hunger.

The young waitress smiled and greeted him, 'Yasas,' as she directed him to a table inside. He positioned himself so he could look out onto the street, he was still hopeful that the girl he now knew as Katerina may make an appearance.

As the young lady placed his order in front of him, she looked up to the television and appeared to be interested in a news article. He watched with her. It showed a reporter on a beach, microphone in hand, pointing towards some trees in a secluded area.

Jordan had a basic understanding of Greek but could not keep up with the speed of the commentary and asked the waitress, 'What's happened, what is he saying?'

'Oh, it's terrible, they've found the body of a young girl on that beach, her throat has been slit.'

'When? Where is the beach?' he asked eagerly.

'This morning, on Amorgos.'

The waitress walked away shaking her head and said something in Greek to the chef behind the counter. He looked back at her and said nothing as he turned his attention to the television screen.

The reporter drew an L-shaped line on his throat and the chef called out. 'Malaka.'

Jordan stood up and went over to talk with the chef. 'Excuse me, what did the reporter just say there?'

The chef explained that the killer had cut the throat of the girl and the incision was L-shaped. Jordan was panicking now. The scar on his waitresses' throat was identical to that which the reporter was describing. This was no coincidence. He paid the bill and stepped out into the warmth of the picture postcard Cycladic street.

Jordan had been sitting on the beach close to the port for half an hour, trying to make sense of everything that had happened since he woke up in Piraeus this morning. This was one of the most tranquil places in the world that he knew, but right now his mind was in turmoil. The murdered girl could not be Katerina, he was trying hard to convince himself. The girl's image had flashed up momentarily on the TV news, her face was blurred out, but she clearly had short blonde hair. What the hell was he doing here? Why him? Perhaps he should just put it down to a weird coincidence and carry on with his planned trip to Skopilos? But he knew himself better than that. He would not be able to let this go, he would have to carry on and find a reason to convince himself to drop it.

—⁓—

Jordan approached the bakery and looked for the entrance to the flat above. He noticed a stairway down a tight side alleyway. As he turned up the alley, an old man sitting on a chair on the street greeted him. 'Kalispera.' He nodded respectfully to the old man and headed to the stairway leading to Katerina's flat. He knocked, and as he waited for a response, he turned to look out at the view. The island that looked like a pregnant lady lying on her back, sat magnificently on the horizon, portraying its mystique to anyone that lived or visited this Island.

The door to the apartment was surrounded by bougainvillea and it almost completely covered a small window to the left side of the door. He brushed the bright magenta flowers away in an effort to take a look inside the flat. As he did so, a key fell out of the bush and landed at his feet. He knocked again, then tried the key in the lock. Jordan pressed the door open slowly and called out, 'Katerina, are you here?' He gave it a few more seconds, then entered. The curtains were drawn but the afternoon sun was shining through and giving the small bedsit a warm feeling. He stepped into the bathroom, looking for any indication that she had been here recently. He felt her towels and they were bone dry, as was the bikini hanging from the shower head. He opened the small cabinet over the sink and it was full of her toiletries. Walking back into the living area, he looked under her bed and could see a large suitcase and a small backpack. Her wardrobe was full of clothes. There was nothing to suggest that she had packed a bag and took off for a few days.

Jordan pulled up a chair by the dressing table next to her bed and noticed the open diary. Her last entry was three days ago. He flicked through the previous pages, she had been making entries daily, but nothing for the last three days. It seemed a bit old fashioned in this day and age for a young person to be keeping a paper diary, quite sweet though. What would it tell him?

He set about finding out what he could, using a translation app on his phone. He started with her last entry, it read, *Pori beach was beautiful today, wonderful waters for swimming. Found a lovely secluded spot but I had a strange feeling that someone was watching me. Creepy! Plenty other beaches to explore.*

He was concerned once again.

Jordan looked at his watch, it was 10pm. He had spent the whole evening slowly deciphering the contents of the diary.

Katerina had left Athens at the beginning of May 2019 and travelled directly to Koufonisia to take up a job as a waitress in a small family restaurant. She was loving the experience and had fallen in love with the Island. She worked split shifts and the working arrangement allowed her to visit the beach every day, usually around the mid-afternoon.

Jordan learnt that Katerina had made friends with another girl that was also working the summer season. Maria worked in the travel agents on the main street in the upper part of the Chora. Maybe Maria could shine some light on where Katerina was? That would have to wait until tomorrow though. He was tired and thought about finding some accommodation for the evening, then decided that under the circumstances, it would probably be okay to crash where he was. He lay fully clothed on top of Katerina's bed and drifted off into a deep sleep.

Saturday 1st June

He was woken at 7am by the sound of a scratching noise. He rubbed his eyes to clear the blur and focused on the sound coming from the bottom of the external door that led to the outside stairway.

A note was being pushed under the door. He jumped up and raced over to retrieve it, trying to be as quiet as he could. As he picked it up, he could hear the sound of someone going down the stairs. He looked at the note quickly and saw that it was signed by Maria.

Without thinking, he opened the door and shouted to the girl descending the stairs, 'Maria, please wait!'

Maria responded in English, 'Who are you..... and where is Katerina?'

'Please, come back up.'

Maria stared back at him, as if he was a stranger asking her to get into a car.

'Sorry, I'm Jordan, I am looking for Katerina.'

The stare continued, 'In her flat?'

'Please, I need to talk to you. Let me explain.'

'You come down here then.'

He descended the stairs and Maria backed off down the alleyway until she was level with the street. Jordan followed her out.

The old man on the chair was sitting in his usual place, he turned to them both and greeted them, 'Kalimera.'

Maria responded, 'Kalimera Dimitris.'

Jordan smiled at the old man and turned towards Maria. She was beautiful, slender, and probably in her mid twenties.

'Go on then, explain.'

He was unsure where to start and just blurted out, 'I am very concerned about Katerina.'

'You are not making sense.'

'Okay.' He thought for a second and continued, 'I met her briefly a few days ago in the restaurant.' It was too early to declare the dream, he would look like an absolute nut case. He stalled and countered her with a question, 'What did your note say?'

She ignored his ploy to evade her line of questioning, 'If you don't start making sense soon, I am going to call the police.'

He took his only option and lied, 'She contacted me to let me know she was in danger.'

'How, when?'

'That's less important right now. I truly believe she is in danger.'

Maria accepted his partial truth, 'I am worried too. I haven't seen her or had any contact with her for three days.'

'Look, maybe this isn't the best time and place to discuss this. Can I meet you later?'

'Sure, call into the travel agents in the upper part of the Chora. It's the only one, you can't miss it.'

CHAPTER TWO

🜚

The Albanian name, Mergim, translates as foreigner or stranger and it best described how Mergim Vokshi had been treated by his mother since he was born. For most of his 27 years he had struggled to understand why his mother behaved the way she did towards him. Showing love one day and resentment the next. He was five years older than his sister, Vlora, and had a very close relationship with her. She understood him better than anyone and was always there when he needed her.

The last contact Mergim had with his mother was six months ago. He had returned to Albania to visit her on her death bed. That is when she had explained her behaviour towards him. It tore him apart. She begged him not to share her story with his sister and he upheld her wish, until his mother passed away one month later.

Saturday 1st June. Afternoon.

Koufonisia

Maria was attending to some customers as Jordan entered her place of work. She looked across at him and gave him a cute smile to acknowledge his presence.

He waited patiently for the customers to leave and asked Maria, 'Is this an okay time to talk?'

'As good as any,' she replied.

He'd had a couple of hours to think about the approach he would take with her. He already knew that
Katerina was not responding on her phone, so he fibbed
again. 'Three days ago Katerina texted me and asked
me to come back to the Island. I had some business to
attend to in Athens and came down as soon as I could.
In truth we barely knew each other, but in the short time
we did, we connected quite strongly.'

'Yes, she is quite naive,' she replied. 'No offense meant.'

'None taken. When I arrived yesterday, I went
straight to the restaurant to see her. That's when I learnt
that she was missing.'

'How did you get into her flat?'

'She told me where she kept a spare key.'

'How strongly did you guys connect?'

'Not as close as you are inferring. I have no idea why
she told me about the key. All I can say is, she did. Do
you have any idea where she could be, Maria?'

Maria shook her head, Jordan could see that she was
tearing up. There is no way that he would mention the
issue of the murdered girl on Amorgos. He did not want
to imply any connection at this point.

'It doesn't look like she has left the Island, Maria,
most of her belongings appear to be in her flat. Could she
have taken a day trip to a nearby Island? Say, Amorgos?'

'I doubt that very much. She wouldn't have time. She
works every day, it's how it is in the summer season.'

Jordan was relieved, 'Then let's check out the possibility that she is still on Koufonisia. Should we start
with the beaches?'

'Yes, good idea. I don't work Sundays, we can go
tomorrow.'

Sunday 2nd June. Morning

Athens

Mergim lifted the girl's suitcase and backpack into the boot of his taxi, then opened the door for her. Sophia slid onto the back seat. She dipped her head so she could look up to the fourth floor flat, her mother was on the balcony waving and blowing kisses to her. She wound the window down and waved back. She would miss her mum tremendously, but she had to do this. She had looked forward to it for so long. Her mum had always said she could go once she was eighteen.

Mergim made eye contact with her in the rear view mirror, 'Where to?'

'Piraeus please, gate E6.'

'Oh, lucky you, where are you heading?'

Sophia replied excitedly, 'Antiparos. I am going to be working the season.'

Mergim smiled to himself. Another young beautiful girl heading for the islands, chasing her dreams. He turned on the digital camera that was set up to capture the image of his passenger.

'Hotel or restaurant?'

Sophia looked into the mirror to reply to him, 'Restaurant. I am so excited.'

'Are you meeting with friends?'

'No, I am hoping to make new friends when I get there.'

Once again, he smiled to himself, 'Sounds wonderful.'

Mergim kept occasional eye contact with her and each time she would smile back politely and provide more personal details about her life and plans. After he dropped her at the port, he joined the queue of taxis waiting for pickups. He downloaded the images from the camera onto his phone and sent them.

—·—

Koufonisia

Maria had arranged to meet Jordan on the pier at the port. They would use the small traditional boat taxi to travel to the isolated beaches. Of the eight beaches, Maria recommended that they visit the most remote three, Pori, Gala and Nero. If Katerina was stranded somewhere, they would be the most likely ones. They should be able to manage that comfortably in one day. She checked her phone, he was late. Then she spotted him running across Ammos Beach, the one adjacent to the port. He was carrying something in his right hand and had a bag strapped across his chest. She could not help having a giggle as he rounded onto the tarmac road and paced up to the pier.

'I'm so sorry Maria,' he panted. 'I checked into a room along by the windmill. The lady wouldn't let me leave without a Greek breakfast this morning.'

'Philoxenia,' she replied.

'I didn't get her name, but she is ever so kind.'

Maria burst out laughing, 'Philoxenia is what we Greeks call the kindness we show to strangers.'

Jordan thought for a second, then joined in with the laughter. He'd heard that word many times, but associated it mainly with names used for hotels.

Maria wiped the tears from her cheeks and motioned towards the water taxi, 'Shall we?'

The first beach was Pori. As they approached, Jordan surveyed the length of the beach with his long range camera lens, taking plenty of shots. 'I don't think we should get off here, Maria. Too many people and the landscape is very low lying. If Katerina was here, I am sure someone would have noticed.'

'I agree, let's stay on until Gala.'

As the boat chugged off, Jordan took in the beautiful colours of the surrounding waters. There was something about the light here that created so many variations in colour. He looked over to Maria, she was conversing with a man sitting next to her. Jordan felt the first pang of butterflies in his stomach, he recognised the feeling. It had not happened much in his life but it was definitely happening now. When should he come clean with her? He decided the sooner the better.

The boat pulled up to the drop off point for Gala Beach and he and Maria were the only ones that disembarked. They stepped off the boat and onto a shingle beach. There was a path leading up to a rocky ridge.

'The view from the top is amazing,' said Maria.

'Then let's go.'

About five minutes into their ascent Jordan stopped, 'Maria, there is something I have to tell you. I have not been absolutely truthful with you.'

Maria looked around, they were alone, apart from a couple swimming in a natural pool below. She felt scared but tried not to show it, 'Carry on then.'

'Katerina did not text me.'

Now she was scared.

'She came to me in a dream.'

'Oh, for fucks sake. I have managed to strand myself with a raving nut case.'

'No, please, hear me out. She had a slash across her throat. It was frightening.'

'Really, I can imagine how scary it was for you,' she replied sarcastically, trying to mask her own fear.

'I know it sounds crazy but I felt compelled to return to Koufonisia. The dream was so vivid. And now a girl has turned up on Amorgos with the same scar.'

Maria's hand was now beginning to shake. Had this guy lured her here on the pretence to look for Katerina, or was he responsible for her friend's disappearance?

Jordan saw the fear in her eyes, 'Oh no, I know what you are thinking. You think I.....' He stepped towards her and she held up her hand. He placed his palms up towards her and stepped back, 'Please Maria. I would rather not be here. I am probably as scared as you. Nothing like this has ever happened to me before.'

'Why didn't you go to the Police?'

'And tell them what? If your reaction is anything to go by, I would be in an asylum by now.'

She laughed, 'And I wouldn't be standing on a rock in the middle of nowhere, crapping myself.'

'Look, if I was the bad guy, why did I call you back from Katerina's flat? Surely I would have just let you go?'

He did have a point. Maria asked him, 'What happened to the girl on Amorgos? I haven't heard about that.'

'I saw it on the news on Friday, but haven't heard anything about it since. Perhaps they have decided to keep it low profile. It's coming up to the major tourist season. That kind of thing can have a bad effect on tourism.' He realised he had not answered her question and continued. 'The girl was murdered, they found her on a secluded beach with her throat cut.'

'Now I understand why you want to check out these beaches. You think the same thing may have happened to Katerina.'

Jordan nodded, 'Yes. I freaked out when I saw the news article. Believe me, this whole thing is weird. I am telling you the honest truth, Maria. I feel like a complete nut job just telling you about the dream.'

Maria smiled at him, 'I will reserve judgement on your sanity for the time being. What's next? What do you want to do now?'

'Let's check out this place considering the two possibilities of an accident or maybe something more sinister.'

Maria smiled and pointed a finger at Jordan, 'By the way, don't ever lie to me again, Malaka!'

Maria and Jordan reached the top of the trail and arrived at the viewing point overlooking Gala Beach. The view was breath-taking from the edge of the rocky ridge, looking down to a cave that arched around and enclosed a beach.

'It's easy to imagine that someone could get hurt climbing down there,' said Maria.

'The thing is, there is so much visibility here and with the amount of tourists visiting, it would be hard to believe anyone could lay injured and not get noticed.'

Maria agreed with a nod and added, 'Plus, it's not a place you could easily abduct anyone. Bearing in mind that Katerina would have only visited the beach in broad daylight.'

'I think we can check this off our list then. Where is the next beach?' asked Jordan.

'Nero. It's on Kato Koufonisia. I think you will find it's much the same as this. No one lives over there. Lots of visitors and nowhere to hide, well, not that I know of anyway.'

'How about we discount that for now then?'

'Okay with me.' Maria looked at Jordan for guidance.

'We can walk back to the Chora from here. It will give us some time to think about our next move.'

They carefully navigated the gravel path down from the viewing point.

'I wondered what you were carrying in your hand when you were racing across Ammos beach this morning,' said Maria.

Jordan raised the tripod and looked at it, 'Oh, this thing. I need it for the distance shots.'

'That's a beautiful camera you have.'

'Yes, I take photos for a living. And you Maria, what do you do when you are not working the summer season?'

'Believe it or not, I have a degree in history. Not that it has led to a good job though. Times are hard in Greece and opportunities are few and far between.'

'So I understand.'

Jordan turned the conversation to the missing girl, 'And Katerina, what about her?'

'As far as I know she has not trained in anything specific. I know how excited she was about working in the restaurant. She is quite a simple, straight forward girl from a village on the outskirts of Athens.'

Jordan thought for a moment and asked, 'Was she on social media?'

Maria laughed, 'I was just starting to get her there.'

'Does she have an account on Facebook?'

'Yes, I set one up for her.'

They had reached the halfway point and Jordan suggested that they take a rest and check out Katerina's

Facebook page. Maria accessed it through her phone. There was no recent activity, but she had uploaded a few pictures. Maria opened them up and they viewed them together. Two with Maria, two selfies and one with another girl.

'Who is that girl with her?' Asked Jordan.

'I have no idea.' Maria hesitated and said, 'No, wait a minute. I recognise that girl. She's been into the office buying ferry tickets on a couple of occasions.'

'How does Katerina know her?'

'That I don't know.'

Jordan asked Maria if he could take a closer look. He took the phone and zoomed in on the image. 'This was taken on a ferry. Must have been when Katerina travelled here to start her job.'

They checked out Katerina's friend listings and Maria was the only one she had.

'I told you, she is a novice with all of this stuff. Looks like she has mastered how to upload pictures though,' said Maria.

'Could be one of those casual meetings you have from time to time. She was probably on a high about her new adventure and got chatting with someone and decided to take a pic.'

'When was that girl last in the office?'

'A couple of days ago, maybe three. It's been busy lately.'

Jordan looked at Maria, 'So around about the time that Katerina went missing?'

Athens

Mergim had finished his shift and was taking his usual Sunday afternoon stroll in the heavily touristic Plaka district of Athens. He loved the anonymity of living in a busy city. Nobody knew him, but he knew people and their little ways. They would reveal so much about themselves and so quickly. Sophia had. She just gushed it all out. He knew her age, where she lived, who she lived with, where she was going and how to find her.

He took a seat in a tavern so he could watch people going about their business. As he drank his raki, he would think about his next trip to the islands. So many to choose from. He planned on spending plenty time down there this summer. There was much to attend to.

―――

Vlora's perspective on many things had changed after Mergim had revealed their mothers dark secret. It triggered many memories from her past and she would frequently go back in her mind to revisit the night that her father left home and deserted his family.

There had been a terrible row between him and her mother. She was only six at the time, but she had clear recall of his volatility and temper. Although he never exhibited any of that directly at her, it was her older brother that seemed to take the brunt of it.

She replayed her memories again. It was late, Mergim was sleeping and she had woken up thirsty and went to get some water. She stopped in the passage way as she heard the shouting. Her father was screaming at her mother, "*How could you keep this from me. I knew the situation when we met, but you lied to me. All of these years you have been living a lie.*" Vlora recalled that her mother just wept throughout his barrage of blame. He went on. "*And that boy, I treated him as my own son. I tell you now, after what you have told me. That boy is evil. You will see, he is evil.*"

That was all that Vlora remembered of that night, her father's words had scared her and she scurried back to her room and pulled the pillow over her ears so she could hear no more.

CHAPTER THREE

Amorgos

Heinous crime in the Cyclades Islands is practically unheard of. So when the body of Emilia Kostas turned up on a beach in Amorgos, it shocked the local community tremendously.

Two Police Detectives from Athens had arrived on the Island shortly after Emilia's body had been discovered, they were to lead the investigation. They had been briefed to keep the murder as low profile as they could. The TV newscast was regretful, it should never have happened. The only reason it did was down to the fact that a news crew was present to cover a festival taking place, the murder story was a totally opportunistic one.

Tracing Emilia's last movements was proving a lot easier than detecting what had happened at the crime scene. Word of her misfortune had travelled fast around the local community in Katapola and her employer came forward immediately. The teenager had only been on Amorgos for ten days and was in the first week of her job as a hotel receptionist. She had finished her shift and told her boss that she was heading out for sundowner drinks.

The hunt for clues at the site of the murder was not going well. Emilia was found under a tree at the extreme end of a sandy cove, close to the waters edge. There were no obvious signs of how she was approached and nothing to suggest that she had put up a fight. Emilia had not been sexually assaulted and the only sign of injury was the incision on her throat. Toxicology reports confirmed that she had been drinking heavily and had possibly mixed sleeping pills with alcohol.

Sunday 2nd June. Afternoon

Antiparos

Sophia was ecstatic, Antiparos was more amazing and idyllic than she remembered. But she was only twelve last time she visited the place for a family wedding. She could not believe that this was going to be her home for the next few months. The trip on the ferry had been spectacular. She had taken so many photos. As she flicked through them, she came across the selfie she had taken with the kind girl that had shared the table with her on the outside deck. Sophia could not remember her name, she was so excited and on such a high, it was hard to recall everything that had happened on the six hour journey.

At first Sophia was disappointed. The recruitment agency had led her to believe that she would be working in a well reputed restaurant, this was not what she saw when she turned up at the address she had been given.

The good news was that the café come bar was on the main street of Antiparos, where most of the nocturnal action occurred. It was 3pm and the place was devoid of customers. As she walked up the short set of stairs and passed by half a dozen sets of tables, a man appeared at the main entrance to the internal sit up bar section.

'Can I help you?' he asked.

'I am Sophia. I was told to ask for Thrassos.'

'I am Thrassos. Yasas Sophia, welcome to your new place of work,' he replied as he stepped towards her and kissed her on both cheeks.

'So I have come to the right place then, this is where I will be working?'

Thrassos noted her slight look of disappointment, 'Yes, and don't worry, you will love it here. We have lovely customers from all over the world and they tip well.'

His comment brought a smile to her face and she felt comfortable with him. He looked as if he was only a few years older than her.

He led her inside, 'Let me get you a coffee and we can discuss your working arrangements.'

She took a seat on one of the bar stools and looked at the décor and the photographs that adorned the interior section. There was the usual stuff that the tourists loved, wooden models of Greek fishing boats and pictures of iconic blue and white buildings. She was warming to the place and starting to imagine herself interacting with customers, this could be fun after all.

Thrassos placed the drinks in front of them, 'Now, we do our best business between 10pm and 4am. That is when we need to have you available for work. Is that okay with you?'

Sophia did not expect to be working that late but replied, 'Yes, that will be fine.'

Thrassos picked up that her words contradicted her facial expression, 'Sorry Sophia, those hours may sound bad, but they do have some advantages.'

She waited patiently for him to deliver the good news.

'It will give you plenty of time to explore the island during day time hours. As long as you are here for the busy period, the rest of the day is yours.'

Two disappointments within half an hour were a lot for her young mind to take and she started to well up with tears.

'Hey, please don't get upset,' said Thrassos as he walked around the bar so he could give her a hug.

'I'll be fine. It's just not what I expected. I thought I would be working in a restaurant, serving lunch and dinner. This is very different.'

'And it's better, believe me. Our tourists come here to drink and have fun, not to complain about food or slow service. You will see, Sophia.' Thrassos asked Sophia to join him at the outside sitting area. He took her to a position so they could look up and down the street. 'What do you see?'

'Lots of bars, restaurants, tables, chairs.....'

Thrassos interrupted, 'Bougainvillea, freshly painted white buildings, sunshine and blue skies. But what you are not seeing are the dreams of the people that come to visit this island. This is a place of escape for them. Escape from work, everyday problems and the complexities of their lives. You will be part of that escape, making this a special time for them.'

Sophia's smile almost broke into a laugh. She gently touched her new friend on the forearm, 'What time do I start work tonight?'

'Get here for 9pm. I will introduce you to some of our nice customers before you begin your work.'

Her employers provided accommodation for Sophia, an apartment located a few streets back from the scenic harbour of Antiparos. It was basic but she had the place to herself. After leaving Thrassos she headed there and decided to take an afternoon nap. As she awoke from her slumber of a few hours, she propped herself up on the bed and looked around her new abode. She recalled what a friend had once said to her. "New places and experiences can appear to be horrible at first but give it some time. They will soon begin to feel normal." As she looked around the room and thought of Thrassos and their conversation, she was slowly coming to realise what her friend had meant.

CHAPTER FOUR

Monday 3rd June

Koufonisia

Jordan pulled the curtains open and climbed back into bed. He rolled on his side so he could watch the morning sun reflect on the sea and the beaches on the pregnant lady island. He had hoped that things may have kicked on with Maria yesterday evening after they returned to the Chora, but she had made her excuses as they parted. He was very attracted to her and he hoped that there would be a chance for him.

He heard people talking directly outside of his room. He jumped out of bed and pulled on his shorts, just as the knock came on the door.

It was a heavily accented Greek male voice, 'Mr Winn, open up please.'

He grabbed a t-shirt from a chair and dragged it over his shoulders. As he opened the door, he saw the land-lady and two policemen looking back at him. 'Morning, how can I help you?'

'Come with us. We need to talk to you.'

'What's this about?'

The response was slightly aggressive, 'Just come with us.' One of the policemen reached in and took Jordan by his elbow.

'Okay, I'm coming.'

The landlady stepped back and watched as Jordan was marched down the stairs and across to the parked police car on the driveway. She was desperate to hear what was being said, but was fearful of the young police officers, they looked angry. She looked on from her kitchen window.

'Where is Katerina Andreou?'

Jordan's heart was racing. What the hell was going on? Why were the cops targeting him in this way? He realised that Maria must have informed the police. 'I don't know where she is. I hardly know her.'

'Then why are you looking for her?' They did not give him time to answer before another question came. 'When did you come to Koufonisia, Mr Winn?'

'On this visit, I arrived on Sunday. But I was here for a few days on another occasion.' Jordan was struggling between answering their questions and restricting what he was telling them.

'Try to be a bit more concise with your answers, Mr Winn. When was that previous occasion?'

'The 26th, I left the island on the 26th. It was a Sunday.'

'Where were you between the 26th and this visit?'

'I took the ferry to Piraeus on the 26th and was in Athens.'

'Can you account for your movements?'

'Yes, I can, but I don't have anything to support it.' Jordan had paid cash for his hotel stays and had no receipts. There is no way that the hotel would support him. Receipts are compulsory in Greece, failure to provide them can have serious repercussions for vendors.

'When did you travel to Amorgos, Mr Winn?'

'Amorgos? Wait a minute. What are you saying? I was never on Amorgos. At least not since last year.'

'Perhaps we should continue our talk at the police station then.'

Jordan's brain was racing to stall his rapidly impending arrest. 'Wait, one moment please. Let me get my camera.'

'Don't fuck with us. What the hell do you want your camera for?'

'I took lots of photos in Athens, they are all digitally time and date stamped. You can check for yourselves.'

The cops stared at each other. They were aware that digital time stamping can be used in legal cases. It may carry some weight in regard to his whereabouts over the last week, but they would need to check the current time setting without him touching the camera. Besides, they needed to exert some more pressure on him. He could sit in a cell while they checked out his camera and figured out their next move.

Jordan sat on the edge of the wooden bench in the tiny police cell and stared down at the concrete floor and thought about Maria. How could she have betrayed him? Why? How had he judged the situation so badly? Surely he had convinced her of his innocence in respect to Katerina's disappearance and the murder of the girl on Amorgos?

It wasn't just the time stamping that saved Jordan from further questioning and suspicion. Several of the photos he had taken in Athens captured billboards that displayed newspaper headlines that corroborated his story of being in Athens for the period under question.

A police Sergeant, accompanied by one of the officers that brought him in, unlocked his cell, 'You are a lucky man, Mr Winn. We are satisfied that you left Koufonisia prior to Katerina's disappearance and we have no reason to believe you visited Amorgos either.'

'Thank you.' Jordan respectfully replied.

'We would appreciate it greatly if you don't take matters into your own hands when you visit our country, Mr Winn. In future, if you have any concerns over the welfare of any of our citizens, then let us know as soon as possible. We don't need an amateur Sherlock Holmes running around our islands.'

'Am I free to go Sir?'

'We will take you back to your hotel to gather your things and hold you until the next north bound ferry comes in. You will have your liberty then. In the meantime, we are going to take a DNA sample from you. I am sure you will not object to that.'

＊＊＊

As Jordan sat on the aft deck of the ferry and watched the low lying island of Koufonisia disappear, he felt sick inside. He reflected on the events of the last few days. It had been one of the most bizarre weekends of his life. He could not get Maria out of his mind, he had fallen for her so quickly. Things could have worked out so badly for him. He was so relieved that they basically kicked him off the island and he was amazed that they allowed him to head off on his own. Perhaps he had convinced them that he was not a threat?

Jordan realised that he was not in possession of a ticket. He had been escorted onto the ferry by the police and directed to the upper decks. His ferry was bound for Naxos, Paros and Piraeus, but without an escort, the destination would be his choice. His perspective on things was changing rapidly, he had to move on and put all of this behind him. Paros was the ideal place to overnight. It was one of the main hubs in the Cyclades for ferries. His mind was made up, he would disembark on Paros, get drunk on ouzo and let this unpleasantness wash over him. Tomorrow was another day.

Monday 3rd June. Evening

Antiparos

Thrassos looked over at Sophia, she returned his look with a beaming smile. The girls were always the same, frightened as hell but desperate for the adventure. He loved the role of playing the big brother. This was her second evening at work in the bar and she was doing just fine.

She stepped up to the bar and placed an order with Thrassos for table five. He asked her, 'What have you got planned for tomorrow?'

'Sleep, sleep and sleep and then to the beach at 3pm I think.'

'There's a really peaceful beach about fifteen minutes walk from where you are staying, once you get to

Fanari, keep going along the coast. It's a tiny bay, not many people know about it.'

'Thanks Thrassos, that sounds ideal.'

—◆◆◆—

Paros

As Sophia came to terms with her new life and settled into her job, Jordan sat in a roof top bar less than 10 kilometres away in Parikia, on the island of Paros. He had gone there to watch the sunset several hours before, but stayed on later to enjoy the Ouzo and to listen in to the conversations on the tables surrounding him. Norwegians, French, Germans and Greeks were providing his evening's entertainment and distracting him from the thoughts that were niggling away in the back of his mind. As the potency of the Ouzo kicked in, he found it harder to keep his subdued thoughts at bay. He kept checking his phone to see if Maria had messaged him and found the decency to explain her betrayal of him. He ordered another drink and tuned into the conversation of the Norwegians on the next table. They were discussing the neighbouring island of Antiparos and how tranquil it was compared to Paros.

'Excuse me, sorry to intervene on your conversation. I heard you talking about Antiparos. Is it worth a visit?'

The young couple were happy to engage with him, 'No problem. It's nice to share with you. It's one of our favourite places. Less busy than here, but still enough going on and plenty to get involved with.'

'And the beaches, how are they?'

'Well that's one of the nicer aspects. They are maybe a little less organised, but there are plenty of choices. Some are very sheltered from the wind too.'

Jordan knew the Cyclades islands well enough to realise that the wind could occasionally spoil a good day on the beach. 'Are they over populated?'

'No, not at all. There are several spots that you could easily have to yourself if you walk down the coast from the harbour.'

Piraeus

Mergim was spending the evening at Flisvos Marina. He loved to look out at the mega yachts that adorned the piers of the upmarket dining and shopping spot. Never in his lifetime could he afford to even pay the berthing fees, let alone own such a beautiful pleasure craft as those that he gazed upon. He did possess maritime skills though. As a young lad in his coastal town of Vlora, the name given to his sister, he had mastered sailing skills to expert level. Dinghy sailing was his love and his ultimate escape from the mood swings of his mother.

He could not wait for tomorrow to come. He was heading to Paros and would be picking up a dinghy there to sail around the island of Antiparos. He was so excited at the prospect of what lay in wait for him.

꙰

CHAPTER FIVE

Tuesday 4th June. Afternoon
Antiparos

Sophia carefully navigated through the slippery rocks on the coastal path and gasped as she saw the natural beauty of the tiny bay that lay ahead of her. This had to be the place that Thrassos had recommended. She had slept through the midday heat and kept to her plan of arriving at the beach for 3pm. This was the perfect place to relax and doze in the dappled sunshine that was filtering through the branches of the Finika trees. She spread her beach towel across a stretch of sand, just in from the waters edge and placed a heavy stone on each corner to prevent the light breeze from flicking it up. Although she had slept well after her shift, she still felt tired and guessed that it was down to the change in her working hours. It would probably take a few days to adjust. As she shifted her weight from her elbows and lay back, she caught sight of a man on a dinghy. He looked like he was having a great time, sailing on the clear blue waters about 50 metres offshore. As she closed her eyes, she knew that she had made the right decision, she was going to love this summer and would hopefully remember it for the rest of her life.

—~~—

Koufonisia

Maria was feeling the first pangs of regret. A young police officer called into the ticket office to thank her for coming to them with the information about the Englishman.

'So, has he left Koufonisia?'

'Yes. That kind of interference in police business is not helpful.'

'Has he been deported?'

'No. Just escorted off the island. We don't believe he is guilty of anything. You know what tourists are like. They think we know nothing here.'

'Any news on Katerina?'

'Nothing to report yet. We have contacted her mother, Katerina is not at home. My advice is don't worry at this stage, it's not unusual for summer girls to run off to have a few days of excitement with someone they meet. There could be a simple explanation for her disappearance.'

Maria knew exactly what he meant. She had developed feelings for Jordan, but those feelings came secondary to the safety of her friend Katerina. She had never intended to direct any blame at Jordan for Katerina's disappearance, she just did not see any sense in not informing the police that her friend was missing. She had hoped that he would understand her actions and come to her to talk about it, she did not consider that the police would expel him in such a way. She picked up her phone, began texting a message to him, then deleted it.

~~~

Antiparos

The Norwegians were not wrong, Antiparos had a totally unique feel. Jordan had arrived there after lunch and spent the late afternoon discovering the beaches close to the port area. Word had it that some of the best ones were located on the south of the island, but he had decided that they could wait for another visit.

He was keen to watch the sun go down from the bar on the North Western point of the Island, another experience recommended by the Norskies. Everywhere seemed to be within walking distance on Antiparos and there was no pressure of crowds anywhere, the buzz was amazing. It was a perfect place to be anonymous and mingle with what appeared to be a cool set of tourists. He arrived at the bar half an hour before sunset time and made sure he was in a prime spot to witness the beautiful light and colour, unique to this part of the world.

He watched a girl walk up to the bar. Where did he know her from? She looked so familiar, but he could not place her. He dismissed his thoughts and efforts to identify her, it was not an unusual thing to run into people he had seen before, especially on the Greek islands where so many people island hop. Sunset was an event and folks were crawling out of the woodwork to witness it. The music in the bar was cranked up to sync with the sun going down, as if the DJ had organised the sunset himself.

Jordan's thoughts drifted to Maria and Katerina as he wandered back through the main street to catch the ferry back to Parikia. The bars and restaurants were crowded and he thought about staying longer to experience the night life, but decided against it. He was not in party mood this evening, if anything, he was feeling melancholy about his unexpected exile from Koufonisia and Maria.

The crossing to Parikia took 25 minutes, the sea was flat calm and Jordan took several photographs of the moonlight as it reflected spectacularly in the water. As he placed his camera back in its bag, he remembered where he had previously seen the girl in the sunset bar. He was sure she was the one on Katerina's photograph, the one she had loaded up to her Facebook page. The same girl that Maria had seen in her ticket office. Why had this girl come into his line of vision? Was this just a weird coincidence?

The ferry arrived and Jordan disembarked. It was a bit too early to retire to the hotel, so he stopped off for a coffee and a night cap in a bar on the main Platia. He took out his phone and nervously compiled the text to Maria. *"I am sorry things worked out the way they did. Very sad that I did not get to speak to you before I was removed from Koufonisia. I think I have just seen the girl on Katerina's Facebook photo, the girl that you saw in your office. Can you please send me a copy of the image? Jordan."* He sent the text and waited for half an hour for a response. When nothing came back, he decided to leave it. He had tried, perhaps Maria wanted nothing more to do with him? He called it a night and made his way back to his hotel.

—⁓—

Mergim lowered the sail on his dinghy and pulled the craft up the beach to ensure the waves would not drag it back out to sea. He would be spending the night in a cave. Today had been good, he was pleased with his efforts.

—⁓—

It was Thrassos' third season in the café come bar. The owner had offered him ongoing employment based on good feedback from the tourists. The boss checked his watch, 'Where is she?'

'I don't know.'

'Call her!'

'I have. She's not answering.'

'Do you know how much it costs me to source new employees Thrassos?'

Thrassos shrugged his shoulders, 'I do my best to help them fit in.'

The boss slammed his fist on the bar and walked away and yelled. 'Malaka!'

❦

CHAPTER SIX

Wednesday 5th June. Morning

Paros

Jordan's phone pinged and woke him at 7am. He reached over and swiped the notification banner on the screen of his phone. Maria had responded and sent the image that he had requested. He was relieved that she was not ignoring him. As he inspected the image and confirmed that it was the girl he had seen, another message came in. *"It is me that should be sorry Jordan. I did not mean to get you into trouble with the police. Sorry x."*

He excitedly typed a reply. *"It's all my fault. It was silly of me to handle things the way I did. Forgive me."* *"By the way, it is the same girl."*

Maria responded with a smiling emoji and a kiss, then typed. *"Call me later please. About 11am if you can."*

───

Antiparos

The sun had crept into the cave and warmed the air inside. Mergim stepped outside and made sure the coast was clear, literally. He returned to the cave and carefully lifted his precious cargo and transferred it to the dinghy. The breeze that would carry him over to the secluded bay on Paros was due to arrive imminently. He would have plenty of time to move his cargo from the dinghy to his blue Hyundai car, then sail up to Parikia to return the dinghy to the rental place. The island bus service could drop him back near his car leaving ample time for him to drive back to the port and make the 1pm ferry sailing.

<center>~~~</center>

Paros

Jordan anxiously waited for his phone to register 11am, then he pressed the call button for Maria.

Maria picked up and said, 'Oriste!'

Jordan recognised the Greek word for, "go ahead, I'm listening," a common way to answer the phone, 'Maria, it's Jordan. How are you?'

She timidly replied, 'I'm good thanks, and you?'

'I am well and glad to be talking to you.'

'Me too. I have some news, it's not good.'

'Please, don't tell me it's about Katerina,' said Jordan.

'No. Well not directly. You know the policemen that came for you?'

'Oh yes. I remember them.'

'I think one of them has a bit of a liking for me. He called into the office this morning. Probably said more than he should of, apparently another girl has gone missing.'

'Oh no. Where?'

'On Antiparos. She was reported missing this morning after she failed to turn up for work last night.'

Jordan had a sinking feeling in the pit of his stomach. 'I can't believe it.'

'Where are you?'

'Paros.' There was an uneasy silence for a few seconds and Jordan picked up on Maria's concern. 'Please Maria, don't jump to any conclusions. I have nothing to do with this.'

'Sorry Jordan, sorry, I .....'

'Yes, I know what you are thinking. But you must trust me.'

'I do, I do.'

'Okay, please hear me out. I was on Antiparos yesterday. That's where I saw the girl. She looked familiar, but I couldn't recall where I'd seen her before. By the time I did, I'd arrived back on Paros. I wished I'd remembered her earlier. I could have asked her about how she knew Katerina.'

'That could have been helpful.'

Jordan went to say something and hesitated.

Maria prompted him, 'Go on. What were you going to say?'

'I was just thinking that it's a bit weird that she was on Antiparos when another girl has gone missing.' He paused and continued. 'I'm probably overthinking it.'

Maria asked him, 'Should I go to the police and show them the photograph?'

'I don't see how you can without bringing me into the conversation.'

'And they would probably want to know what you were doing on Antiparos, when another girl has gone missing there.'

'You've got it. Besides, there is nothing to suggest that the girl is guilty of anything. She may have a perfectly good explanation for everything.'

'So what do we do?'

'Can you trace your ticket sales to individuals?'

'Only by the name they give me at the time of sale. We don't ask for any form of identification. It's only so we can put a name on the ticket when we print it off. Nobody on the ferry checks anyway.'

'Give it a go, please Maria.'

'Will do. I must go now. I will text the name to you if I can find it.'

'Are we friends again?'

'Of course. Talk soon, filakia.'

Jordan looked up the word filakia, it meant "kisses." He smiled to himself at the thought of her sending him a kiss.

An hour later, he received a text from Maria. It read, "*V.Vokshi*." He immediately checked out the name on social media and it came up with scores of individuals. Without some sort of filter, just having the name would not be helpful. However, he was able to deduce that the name was of Albanian origin.

Maria was correct, her admirer, Mikalis, had told her too much. The Southern Aegean authorities were trying their best to restrict the flow of information about the missing girls. They had to limit any potential damage to the tourist industry and had succeeded to a degree in respect to the murder of Emilia. Social media could be a great tool to solicit help from the public, but in this situation, it was their biggest concern. Record numbers were expected to visit the region this summer, there was much at stake. The girls had to be found safe and well and quickly. Further to that, an arrest would also go a long way to calm the nerves of those concerned.

Now that Jordan had confirmed who the girl was, he was kicking himself for missing the opportunity to talk to her. Returning to Antiparos to try and track her down would be a huge risk. The message from the police was clear, "Keep out of our affairs." Not only that, he was pretty sure that they would not need much of an excuse to bring him in again, especially if he turned up at another crime scene. He took a table at the café closest to the Paros ferry terminal. From there he could see all the ferry comings and goings to the island. The café was full of travellers, patiently waiting for their ferries to arrive. Maybe Ms Vokshi would move on from Antiparos and show up here? As the caffeine kicked in, he had a thought. He called Maria, 'Hey Maria. Just a quick one. What ferry company did our Ms Vokshi use?'

'Let me check.' Maria located the transaction on her computer. 'Sea Jets. All three tickets were for Sea Jets.'

'Great, thanks Maria. I will call you later. Yasas.'

Jordan walked over to the ticket office a few metres from his table and studied the ferry departure board. There were two Sea Jet departures due for today, luckily neither of them had left yet, but both were due to sail in the next 45 minutes. If the Vokshi girl was going to depart Antiparos and use her ferry of choice, then it was a good bet that she would be taking one of those. He may still get his opportunity to talk to her.

The ferry terminal had quite a good queuing arrangement. Four covered lanes were used to separate ferry passengers based on the destination of the appropriate ferry. Jordan settled back in his chair and used his long range camera lens to home in and take random photos of the passengers standing in line for the Sea Jets lanes. There was only a handful of people there, but no Ms Vokshi yet. He watched a large blue ferry arrive and masterfully berth its stern against the pier. It was bound for Piraeus, via Naxos and Mykonos, and would depart shortly before the Sea Jets. He focused in on the blue Hyundai as it drove up the ramp, the powerful zoon on his camera allowed him to see that the driver was wearing a red Olympiacos cap, it amused him and he captured the image. He was amazed at how quickly the ferries performed their turn around in these ports. It was all very skilful and well managed.

When he turned his attention back to the queues, they had begun to fill up. It was difficult to pick out individuals with his camera zoom now. He could see the Sea Jet ferries arriving, he had to get closer to get a better view. He pulled out some coins and left them next to his receipt on the table. By the time he crossed the road and headed to the passenger lanes, the entrance had become congested with tourists and their suitcases. He could see her, the Vokshi girl had arrived, she was mingling with the crowds as they interwove to line up with their ferry lanes. He had to get close enough to confirm that it was her. The two Sea Jet lanes were in the centre section. One lane was for Naxos and the other was for Santorini. He thought she took the one for Santorini, he would have to move to catch up. But it was becoming difficult to get through the crowds, it appeared that lots of people had left it to the last minute to join their queues. The Santorini ferry was going to be the first one to depart and the gate at the front of the lane had opened allowing passengers to make the short walk up to the boarding ramp. He had to hurry. He pushed his way past an older couple that were taking forever with their bags and he moved as fast as he could to catch up with the girl. He was panicking now as he realised that he had lost sight of her. As he reached the gate at the front of the lane to Santorini, a port policewoman asked him to show his ticket. He could go no further. As he turned to walk back down the lane, he looked through at the crowd of people in the Naxos queue. He saw her. He had picked the wrong lane. She would be too far away to hear his call, so Jordan just watched as she moved off and boarded the ferry to Naxos.

Jordan texted Maria, "*My hunch almost paid off. She turned up to catch a ferry and I couldn't get near to her. I messed up with the queues. She boarded the ferry to Naxos.'*

Maria replied. 'Wow, clever man! What a shame. At least you tried.'

"*It was definitely her though.*"

"*Mikalis the cop is meeting me for a coffee during my afternoon break.*"

Jordan experienced his first feeling of jealousy in a long time. Perhaps his feelings were one sided? Who was he to sweep this young Greek goddess off her feet anyway? He replied, "*Enjoy. Try and pick his brains without giving anything away.*"

She replied with a single "thumbs up" emoji.

Koufonisia

Mikalis was a young naive cop, not long out of training school. He had been stationed on Koufonisia to learn the ropes and was loving the posting. He was trying to be as cool as he could in front of Maria, but it was not working. He was breaching confidentiality and demonstrating a lack of professionalism.

Maria was milking what she could from him, 'I bet your parents are proud of you Mikalis, being involved in this huge case on the islands?'

'Oh no. They don't know anything about it. I'm not allowed to tell anyone.'

Maria smiled, 'I am really worried about my friend Katerina. Have you any leads?' She added a deliberate pause for effect. 'Sorry, I know you can't talk about it. I shouldn't have asked you.'

He waited for a moment, smiled at her and replied, 'That's okay, you are kind of involved anyway. We have nothing to go on yet. The only thing linking the cases is that all the girls are here working the summer season. We think they are being targeted.'

'Targeted?'

He realised he had alarmed Maria, 'We are doing everything we can. We track their phones and monitor all of their social media feeds.' He was keen to show off and used his phone to log onto Sophia's Facebook account. 'We get special access to their online stuff. Look, this is the girl that was reported missing today.' He moved around to show Maria the contents on Sophia's Facebook page. 'She has loaded up a lot of photos. She must have been so excited about coming to the islands.'

Maria placed her finger on the screen and flicked through the photos. There was one of a lady waving from the balcony of some flats. A picture taken from the back seat of the yellow taxi, no driver, just a shot through the windscreen and an Olympiacos cap on the dashboard.

Maria continued flicking through and stopped suddenly when she reached the photos that had been taken on a ferry, 'Ela!' Maria was looking at a photo of Sophia and the Vokshi girl.

'What's up? What have you found?' said Mikalis.

'This girl.' Maria took out her phone, opened the image of Katerina and the Vokshi girl and placed her phone alongside his. 'This is the same girl. She was on Antiparos on Tuesday night.'

'How do you know that?'

As Maria spoke the words, she realised that she had made the gaffe. There was no way out for her, she had to drop Jordan in it. She reached over and touched his hand. 'Can I trust you, Mikalis?'

'Trust me with what? I am a policeman Maria. Tell me how you know this!'

'Someone told me.'

'Who?'

'It was Jordan. The Englishman that I told you guys about.'

Mikalis rolled his eyes and pulled his hand away from hers. 'He was warned to keep out of our affairs. Now you are telling me that you and he are interfering in this together.'

His reaction angered her, 'We are not interfering in anything. He recognised her, it was a simple coincidence. Right place, right time.'

'And you honestly believe that?' It was Mikalis's turn to get jealous. 'Are you and this English person involved?'

Maria stood up to leave. 'What business is that of yours?'

'Oh, don't you worry. I can make it as much of my business as I want.'

Maria turned and walked away. This meeting and her judgement of the cop had been a huge mistake. What was she going to say to Jordan?

—◊◊◊—

Naxos

On arrival in Naxos, Vlora Vokshi made the short walk to the end of the pier and picked up her motor scooter. It would take her 30 minutes to reach the villa in Halki. She had visited the village in March and secured a medium term rental deal for cash only with the owner. The mountain village was ideal for her needs. Vlora worked hard to maintain her anonymity in the village, and the location of the villa on the outskirts made that task easier.

—◊◊◊—

Koufonisia

Maria had been back at work for a couple of hours and was reflecting heavily on her meeting with Mikalis when the call came in from Jordan. 'Hi Maria, how did it go?'

'Not good Jordan, I am sorry to say.' She sheepishly replied.

'Okay, let me have it.'

'I think I have dropped you in it. I couldn't help it. I reacted to something that we discovered and before I knew it, I gave it away that you were on Antiparos.'

'How far has it gone? I mean, who knows I was there?'

'As far as I know, it's only the cop, Mikalis.'

'Are they going to come looking for me?'

'I don't know, I don't think so. To be honest, I think he is only jealous of my relationship with you, rather than thinking that you are messed up with the disappearances.'

Jordan was touched by Maria's words. It was nice to know that she had a relationship with him. 'Try and reconnect with him. Find out where he is with things. At the end of the day, I am totally innocent of any wrong-doing. That has to count for something.'

'Sure. Leave it with me. I will accidently on purpose bump into him somewhere.'

'Great, I am going to lie low for a couple of days. I'll stay on Paros and head over to the town of Naousa and try and pick up some casual photography work. Good luck.' Jordan was about to hang up and realised that Maria had not revealed what she and the cop had discovered. 'Oh, by the way, what was it that you found out?'

'The new missing girl has also met our Ms Vokshi. She has a selfie of them together on her Facebook page.'

'Really?'

'Yes. Mikalis accessed her account and I found the photo myself. I freaked out when I saw it and couldn't help blurting out that you had seen the girl on Antiparos.'

'And rather than take that information for what it was, he was more interested in jumping to conclusions about me?' Jordan thought for a moment. 'Look Maria love, sounds like he is focusing on the wrong things. I think you may be right, he probably has the hots for you. Let's hope that's all it is anyway.'

The word "love" jumped out of Jordan's comment. She liked it. 'As I say, leave it with me. Try and enjoy your time in Naousa. Yasas. Filakia.'

He smiled and replied. 'Filakia.'

Mikalis knew he had over-reacted. The last thing that he wanted was to push Maria away. He had to learn to control his jealousy. Why did he ever think mixing business with pleasure could be a good thing? All was not lost though, there would be other ways to impress Maria.

He took the new information to his Sergeant. Putting the Englishman aside, it was quite suspicious that both missing girls had a photograph taken with the same girl and that she was spotted on Antiparos when Sophia went missing.

His Sergeant did not think that was so incredible though. 'That proves nothing Mikalis. These young girls spend so much time on social media now and what's more, it's only a couple of photographs.'

'Sorry Sergeant, I just thought it was worth a mention.'

'Sure.' He touched the young cop on his shoulder. 'Let's leave the detective work to the Detectives. You carry on with visiting the hoteliers on the island. They can be our best eyes and ears out there. Ask them to be extra vigilant and to look out for any guests that may be of interest to us.'

The conversation lifted Mikalis. He would wait a while and go back to Maria with the news that her friend was not under suspicion and that her information had been useful to the investigation. Perhaps that would put him in a good light with her.

CHAPTER SEVEN

✤

Thursday 6th June

Athens

Vasilis Kostas had not seen his daughter since she was five years old. He cried for one hour, wrapped in the arms of his wife, after the Melbourne police had informed him of her death. He would be making the long flight from Australia to Athens alone. His new family knew little of his life before and understood that this was something he had to do on his own.

The authorities had released Emilia's body and her mother made the arrangements to bring her beloved daughter home. The funeral would be traditional Greek Orthodox. Emilia would lay in rest at the funeral home for two days, then she would be brought back to the small apartment she had called home for most of her life. It was comforting for her mother to know that Emilia would be surrounded by her family and friends during the short procession to her local Church for the funeral service.

Vasilis went over the discussion with the police officers that had broken the news to him. They did not provide any detail of how Emilia's life was taken, but they went out of their way to comfort him with the fact that the crime was not a sexually motivated one. Although that was a relief in itself, it did not lessen the hammer blow that he felt at losing her this way, discovered all alone on a remote beach. He had to find out more about what had happened to Emilia, but not from his ex-wife, or her family. There was no love lost there. The divorce had been as acrimonious as it gets. In fact, he was dreading the thought of being in close proximity with any of those people. In return, he was no favourite of theirs. The sooner he returned to Australia, the better.

Vasilis picked up the hire car on arrival at Eleftherios Venizelos airport. Within seconds of switching his phone on, he received the text message from his oldest friend, Dimitris, informing him of the funeral home address. He called ahead to the funeral home to request a private viewing with his daughter.

Vasilis entered the tiny room and the attendant closed the door after him, leaving him to say farewell to his daughter. He would not have recognised her if she had passed him on the street, but this was his baby girl. He bent over and kissed her cold brow. He ran his fingers over her shoulder and reached up to cradle the side of her face in his warm hand. It was then that he saw the scar on her throat. He pulled his hand away and reeled back in shock.

As he stepped outside and onto the street, his heart was racing and his head was thumping, he touched his brow and he was sweating. He crossed over the busy side street, and as he closed in on his hire car, he noticed something tucked under his windscreen wiper. 'Not a fucking parking ticket,' he said to himself. As he got closer, he could make out that it was an envelope, he removed it and it felt like a card. Vasilis opened the envelope and slid the card out. It was a sympathy card, but the sender had crossed out the word 'sympathy'. He expelled the words. 'What the fuck?' His hand was shaking as he opened the card to read the text inside. *"You won't be able to run from this! Hope your conscience is plaguing you, for this and for what is about to come!"* He banged his fist on the top of the roof of the car and slipped the card into his jacket pocket. His head was spinning, he was in no fit state to drive. He looked up and down the street, he was alone, except for an old lady pushing a shopping trolley. Nobody was watching him. He needed time to calm down and think. He walked up to a café a few metres up the street and took a seat at a table outside. It was already 28 degrees and the jet lag was starting to kick in. Perhaps a double Greek coffee would help him focus his mind? As he waited for his order to come, his thoughts drifted back to Emilia, the scar on her neck, and the words written on the card.

Naxos

Vlora's phone buzzed, she had new mail. She opened the attachment and viewed the video. She texted her brother. *"Where?"*

"Naxos."

"No way!"

"Why?"

"We agreed, the main ferry hubs have to be sacred ground."

"Okay. Lucky girl then! Leave it with me, let's see what tomorrow brings."

Vlora responded with a thumbs up emoji.

Koufonisia & Paros

Maria called Jordan, 'Kalimera Jordan, ti kanis?'

'Maria. Poly kala, efharisto.'

'Very good, you are improving. Quick question. Are you free tomorrow?'

Jordan tried to contain his excitement, 'I can be. Why?'

'How about I meet you on Irakleia? I have a free day. Can you get there for lunch time?'

'I'll check the ferry times, but I am sure that will be okay.'

'Great, I will explain everything when we meet. Gotta go. Yasas, bye for now.'

Whatever Maria had to tell him was obviously important, but the fact that they were meeting was great news for Jordan. Had she not been in so much of a rush, he could have asked her how long she intended to stay. He would just have to play it by ear, worst case he could overnight on Irakleia and travel back to Paros on Saturday. She wanted to see him and that was good enough for now.

Friday 7th June

Athens

Emilia's mother hated her ex-husband, but today she would have to bottle her feelings. It would be more difficult for her brother Manolis, Emilia's Uncle. The entire family was concerned about how he would react when he came face to face with Vasilis. When Vasilis deserted his family, he left them with nothing. He had met an Australian tourist, packed his bags and joined his new woman in her travels around Europe. Within a few months, they had set up home in Melbourne and Vasilis began proceedings to divorce his Greek wife and forget his old life. Now he was back on Greek soil for the first time, his friend Dimitris had warned him not to expect an easy ride.

Vasilis had his suspicions about the sender of the card and Manolis was top of the list. However, there was another factor that could exclude his ex-brother-in-law as the culprit, but there was no way that he could share that with anyone, including Dimitris. If Manolis was the responsible party, then Vasilis Kostas would make him pay for it, he would just have to choose the right moment.

Irakleia

It was Jordan's first visit to Irakleia. It was one of the best harbour scenes he had seen in his travels to this part of the world. Beautiful clear blue and turquoise water and a gorgeous sandy beach as a backdrop to the peaceful bay. He took as many photos as he could before hurrying down the stairways to disembark from the ferry. As he walked along the pier, he could see Maria waving at him from the water's edge on the beach.

As he stepped down onto the sand, Maria came over to greet him. 'Please forgive me Jordan, I seem to be making a habit of getting you into trouble.'

He laughed and she moved over to hug him. She took him by the hand and they walked over to a shady spot under a tree at the rear of the beach.

'This place is awesome,' he said.

'I love it. I thought it would be a good place for us to meet.'

She unrolled a blanket and laid it out on the sand, then placed a picnic hamper in the centre of it. 'Please, sit. Are you hungry?'

'Starving.'

Maria started to unpack the hamper. Tzatziki, meat balls, marinated octopus, fava beans and bread. 'Please, eat.'

Jordan tucked in. 'Wow, this is great.'

'You are welcome. I hope it makes up for things?'

'More than enough, Maria. Speaking about things, how are they?'

Maria explained how Mikalis had called into her office, apologised to her and updated her on events. She satisfied Jordan that he was no longer of interest to the police, although a return to Koufonisia was not advised for now.

'They don't think the murder and the missing girls are connected. Emilia, the murdered girl, had injuries that they would typically associate with a serial killer. Apparently, the police have performed thorough searches on Koufonisia and Antiparos. They seem to think the missing girls would have shown up by now if a serial killer was involved. Emilia was clearly meant to be found. It's beginning to look like Katerina and Sophia have been taken.'

'Are you saying they could still be alive?'

'We can only hope, Jordan.'

'Looks like Mikalis has loosened his tongue again.'

Maria laughed and replied. 'He had no option, I told him I wouldn't speak to him again if he didn't keep me informed.' She waited a few seconds and looked Jordan in the eyes. 'Don't worry Jordan. I am not interested in Mikalis.'

Jordan smiled. 'That's good to know.'

The revelation caused a moment of silence to fall between them. Maria filled the gap. 'It is Emilia's funeral today.'

Athens

Vasilis and Dimitris waited for the procession to move off before stepping into line just behind Emilia's mother, who was being supported by her brother. Manolis looked over his shoulder and made eye contact with Vasilis, who in turn stared back and eventually broke off the uneasy interaction after a few seconds.

Dimitris' position was uncomfortable, he was close to Emilia's family but also had a strong bond with Vasilis, despite their distant relationship. He knew there was no chance of any kissing and making up, if anything he would do his best to play the peacekeeper.

Vasilis was trying to manage his internal conflict of despair, guilt, anger and desperation to confront Manolis.

The smell of the incense spilled out onto the street from the door of the church. The aroma from the candles and the chanting welcomed her family and friends into the church, as Emilia lay in her open casket to allow them to pay their last respects to her.

Dimitris guided Vasilis towards a row of chairs at the rear of the church and away from his ex-wife. Manolis witnessed the gesture and acknowledged Dimitris' action with a discrete nod.

—∽∿∽—

Irakleia

Jordan and Maria finished their lunch and headed along the main road that wound up a hill and away from the port. They sat at a table in a roof top bar that looked out over the bay.

'So what do we do now, Maria?'

'Well, the cops seem to think our Ms Vokshi's presence on Antiparos and the coincidental photos are not important, but my gut feeling is that they are.'

'Mine too.'

'Did the cops check Emilia's Facebook for a photo?'

'Yes. There wasn't one. I think if they'd found one, they would have been more interested in Ms Vokshi.'

'Okay, I get that logic.' Jordan thought for a moment and continued. 'Look, we have to believe that Katerina is just missing and we should keep looking for her. If we work on the premise that the Vokshi girl is involved, until we prove different, we should try and track her down. Everything we have learnt about her so far suggests she is hanging around the Cyclades, so she must have a base somewhere. I think Naxos is worth a visit.'

'Do you have time for this Jordan, I mean, don't you have to work?'

Jordan smiled, 'I am doing okay for money. I have some passive income from royalties from some of my photos. Besides, I like riding on ferries.'

Maria laughed and leant over and kissed him on his cheek. 'Thank you.'

The voyage to Koufonisia would only take 20 minutes for Maria. She had really enjoyed meeting with Jordan. The disappearance of her friend was rocking her emotionally and Jordan's support was helping to settle her nerves. As much as she would have liked to join him with the search, she had a job and could not just walk away from it. She believed the police were doing all they could to look for the missing girls, but they were certainly not reaching out to the public for help. She liked Jordan and wondered when they would see each other again, she hoped it would not be too long.

Athens

Vasilis insisted on standing at the graveside when his daughter was laid to rest. He had agreed to keep a low profile in the church, but not here. This was his last farewell and he did not care who he upset. At one point he made eye contact with Emilia's mother, her stare was cold and empty, that did not surprise him. He disengaged his contact immediately, he bore her no ill. He accepted that the marriage breakdown was down to him and she was the victim of his decision. But today they were burying their child. Deep inside he felt a need to comfort her, but that would not happen.

As the burial concluded and the attendees left the cemetery, Manolis left his sisters' side and walked towards Vasilis and Dimitris. 'Dimitris, please join us at the wake.' Then he pointed at Vasilis. 'But don't bring him.'

Vasilis responded by taking a step towards Manolis and Dimitris restrained him. 'Leave it!'

CHAPTER EIGHT

✿

Saturday 8th June

Naxos

Naxos has several villages, Jordan decided to start with the biggest ones first. He worked on the theory that if Ms Vokshi was based on Naxos, then she would need supplies, so supermarkets would be a good place to start. He had been to Naxos many times and knew that there were about five supermarkets spread around The Chora, the main town that is set around the port. He systematically worked them all, using the photo of Ms Vokshi on his phone to show to the staff on duty. The supermarket owners and their employees tended to work long hours, so there was a good chance of recognition if she was visiting their store. He drew a blank in The Chora, maybe it was too busy for Ms Vokshi? Too many tourists? Perhaps the mountain villages of Filoti, Halki and Apeiranthos would be more to her liking?

He hired a motorbike and headed off on his venture to the more remote villages on the island. Halki was first and came up with nothing. The next village was Filoti and he hit lucky at the second supermarket.

'Yes. I recognise her, she comes in here. She was here yesterday,' said the assistant.

'Do you know if she lives in the village?'

'I have no idea, but she comes in once a week. Has done for a few weeks now.'

Jordan thanked the young girl working the till and stepped out onto the main road that ran up through the village. Filoti was a fair size, he would have to be very lucky to randomly come across her. At the very least he had confirmed that she was using the island as her base. It was a start.

He crossed the road and sat in a cafe facing the supermarket, as he pondered his next move and ordered a coffee. The waiter seemed friendly, it was worth a try, so he showed him the photo. 'Excuse me, have you seen this woman before?'

'Sure. She comes here for lunch occasionally.' The waiter joked, 'Why, has she robbed you?"

Jordan utilised the opportunity to adopt a lie, 'Yes. I did some work for her and she ran off without paying me.'

'Malaka,' he smiled.

'Can you do me a favour? If she comes in again can you text me? Please don't let her know that I am looking for her though.'

'Sure. Nobody likes getting ripped off.'

About 20 metres down the road from the café, Jordan located a small guest house. It had a vacant room with a balcony looking out on to the street. It was perfect for his needs, he booked it for a few days. He would be able to monitor the café and the supermarket from the balcony, along with the chance of an alert from his new friend, the waiter. Jordan now fancied his chances of finding Ms Vokshi. It was a bit premature to update Maria, he did not want to get her hopes up yet. Jordan liked the feel of Filoti, it was a typical Greek village surrounded by hills and valleys with iconic blue and white churches strategically placed on high points around the village. There were plenty photographic targets here to keep him busy whilst he waited for the mysterious Ms V to make an appearance.

Vlora was scouring newspapers and online news feeds on a daily basis. She was growing increasingly frustrated at the realisation that news of the missing girls and the murder was being intentionally suppressed. She was intelligent enough to know why, but it did not help the cause. Things had to be accelerated. She made the phone call to raise her concerns.

Athens

Manolis took the short walk from his apartment to his parked car. As he opened the door, he felt the blow to the side of his neck. His whole body felt weak and he sank to his knees. Vasilis bundled him into the rear of the car and picked the car keys up from the pavement, before entering the car from the other side and joining his ex-brother-in-law on the rear seat.

Manolis straightened up and rubbed the side of his neck. 'What the fuck!'

Vasilis took the card from his pocket and held it in front of Manolis, 'Exactly. What the fuck is this? And what is meant by the phrase, "What is about to come? Malaka!'

Manolis was genuinely confused. 'I have no idea what you are talking about.'

Vasilis grabbed him by the throat and pressed on the side of his neck where he had inflicted the blow. 'Not good enough. Think again.'

'I am telling you Vasilis. I have no idea what you are talking about or who gave you that card, but it was not me. I fucking hate your guts, but that crap is sick.'

Vasilis released his grip on him and sat back and looked at the card. He slid it back in his pocket and got out of the vehicle. He leaned in through the open door and said. 'If I find out you are lying, I will kill you.' Then he slammed the door and walked away.

Dimitris patiently waited for the arrival of his friend at the harbour front bar in Mikrolimano. The place was very popular with the local community and the smooth jazz music and tasty furnishing was a refreshing change from the traditional blue and white décor that was exhibited just about everywhere. Vasilis had showed him the sympathy card and told him that he was going to confront Manolis about it.

As Vasilis arrived and sat at the table, Dimitris edged a cold bottle of beer towards him. 'So, how did it go?'

'He said he had nothing to do with it.'

'Do you believe him?'

Vasilis shook his head. 'Don't know.'

Dimitris held out his hand. 'Let me see the card again.'

Vasilis handed it over and Dimitris asked him. 'What do you think it means, when it says, for what is about to come?'

'Sounds like some kind of threat. But something that is related to my conscience.'

'Your conscience. What could that be?'

Vasilis lied. 'I have no idea.' He took a long drink of his beer and asked. 'How much do you know about Emilia's murder? I saw the scar on her throat. What do you know about that?'

'When they found her on the beach, her throat had been cut in an L shape. Her artery had been cut and she bled out where she lay, apparently.'

Vasilis turned his head sideways and reflected on what his friend had just said. 'Thanks Dimitris. I needed to know.'

'How long are you staying?'

'A few more days. I've been away from Greece for a long time, it's good to be home and good to catch up with you again.'

'Yamas,' said Dimitris as he raised his beer.

Vasilis headed off back to his hotel. He was staying in central Athens. As he stepped into his hotel room, he saw the envelope lying on the floor, it had been pushed under his door. He pulled out the note from inside. *"Go to the police and ask them about the two girls that are missing. Koufonisia and Antiparos! You have 24 hours or another girl will be taken. Have no doubt, they will suffer the same fate as your daughter."*

He let out a deep breath and sat on the edge of the bed. What was going on? Was this some sick person trying to blackmail him? His wife in Australia was a wealthy woman, maybe someone had found that out and was trying to exploit them in his grief stricken state?

It was already Sunday morning in Melbourne. Vasilis called his wife, and after a few minutes of pleasantries he got to the real reason for the call, he had to find out if anyone had been in contact with her in relation to what was happening to him here. He diplomatically hedged about with some questions and ascertained that no one had, well not yet anyway.

CHAPTER NINE

⚘

Sunday 9th June

Naxos

The sound of church bells roused Jordan, he climbed out of bed and pushed the window shutters open. The light and warmth flooded into his room. His phone beeped, a text had just come in. *"Yasas. Your lady friend is in the supermarket."* He had to think for a minute, but then he realised that the text was from the waiter. He hurriedly pulled on his clothes and ran downstairs and out onto the street. He walked past the supermarket and looked in without showing himself to the unsuspecting Ms V. Once he confirmed it was her, he headed back down the street and straddled his motorbike and waited for her to come out. She placed three carrier bags in the storage box at the back of her motor scooter and headed down the hill that exited the village. Jordan followed her, keeping a discrete distance behind her. They arrived at the village of Halki and Ms V. slowed down and turned into the driveway of a villa. Jordan continued riding and stopped further up the road. He was ecstatic, he was sure that she had not seen him, and now he knew where she was staying. He found a convenient spot behind some trees, across the road from the villa, then he took out his camera and snapped a few shots of the front of the villa and her scooter. The shutters were closed, so there was no chance of any images through the windows. As he clicked away, the front door opened and Ms V. stepped out. She walked over to her scooter and placed a small backpack in the storage box. Before she went back inside, he managed to get a few images of her without being noticed.

Vlora received the latest video clip from Mergim, along with the text. *"Today. Ios. Dep: Naxos13:00hrs. Andrea."*

Jordan had a feeling that Ms V would be on the road again soon, loading the backpack was the clue. He made his way back to his motorcycle and waited. It took her half an hour to make an appearance again. This time she was heading towards Naxos Chora. Once again, he kept a discrete distance away and followed her down to the port area. On arrival, she parked up and headed to a ticket office, he followed her in and looked at some brochures on the counter as he listened to her discussion with the assistant behind the counter. She was taking the ferry to Ios at 13:00 hrs today and she paid extra to include her motor scooter. He gave her a few minutes to exit the ticket office and he purchased a ticket for the same ferry.

Athens

Dimitris' phone rang, it was Vasilis. Dimitris asked him how things were.

'Not good. There was another note last night.'

Vasilis went on to explain how he found the note and what it said.

'They want you to go to the police? What's going on, Vasilis? Is there something I don't know about here?'

'No, you know everything about me.'

Dimitris replied. 'This is all very strange Vasilis.'

Vasilis asked. 'Have you heard anything about missing girls on the islands?'

'No, but let me ask around. I have a cop friend. He may know something.'

'Thanks Dimitris. I need all the help I can get right now. Please be discrete though.'

'Sure.'

Naxos & Ios

Jordan parked his bike close to Ms V's scooter and followed her out of the garage space and up to the passenger decks. She had her phone in her hand and kept looking at the screen as she walked through the internal seating section and out onto the open deck at the rear of the ferry. She stopped and visually scanned the people sitting at the tables on the aft deck, after a few seconds she seemed to identify the person she was looking for. Jordan watched on as Ms V. took a photograph and studied the image. She slipped the phone in her pocket and walked over to the girl she had just photographed and asked her if she could sit at her table. The girl nodded to approve the request and Ms V. smiled and took a seat next to her. Jordan found a vantage point on an empty table a few metres away and began taking a few photos as the girls chatted together. They seemed to be getting on very well, so much so that Jordan thought that they possibly knew each other, but the request for the seat from Ms V discounted that. If she knew her, she would not have politely requested to sit at her table the way she did. After 45 minutes or so, the girls lifted their phones and took a selfie of themselves. Jordan felt a shiver run down his spine as he recalled the images of Katerina and Sophia with Ms V. He now believed that the girl was being targeted.

The announcement came over the tannoy that the ferry was approaching Ios and advised disembarking passengers to make their way down to the garage to be ready to leave. Jordan watched on as Ms V stood up first and said her farewell to the young girl. Passengers were converging on the stairways leading down to the garage and he kept a safe distance behind Ms V, he had to follow her closely without being noticed. The other girl was out of sight now, it would be impossible to tail both, besides, it was Ms V's movements that were of more interest to him.

The sensation in the garage always amused and excited Jordan. The ferry seemed to lunge over to one side as it spun round to position its stern to line up with the pier. At the same time, the sirens would be wailing as the huge ramp opened allowing blue sky and the first view of the port to appear. The foot passengers were always the first to disembark, followed by bikes, cars and transport vehicles. Jordan sat on his motorcycle, he was placed nicely to view Ms V. As the ferry righted itself and the ramp was landed, he could pick out the other girl, she was standing towards the rear of the hundred or so passengers eagerly waiting to step out onto Ios. He could also see that Ms V had her in her sights. The crew gave the signal for passengers to make their way down the ramp. By now, the port was on full view. A stunning blue sky was contrasting with the white buildings and semi arid hills that cradled around the scenic harbour.

Jordan fell in behind Ms V as they rolled off the ramp onto the pier and into the warm sunshine. The port police were waving their arms and using their whistles to move the crowds and vehicles away from the pier as fast as they could. Ms V was carefully navigating through the crowds and, at the same time, maintaining sight of the girl. It only took a few minutes for the girl to locate a vacant taxi. As the taxi pulled away, Ms V followed and Jordan made up the rest of the small convoy as it headed out of the port and climbed up into the hills. Within fifteen minutes, they arrived at a turn off for Mylopotas beach. The view was sensational as they wound down the steep incline to the vast arc of beach and its many hotels. They reached the beach area and the taxi slowed down, the girl had reached her destination. Jordan stopped and watched Ms V as she overtook the taxi when it pulled into a beach resort. She rode on for a few metres, made a u-turn and sped past him and back up the hill that they had just descended. It appeared her reconnaissance mission was over for now.

Jordan dismounted and walked into the beach front bar that he had conveniently parked next to. He ordered a beer and called Maria to brief her on his discoveries.

Maria excitedly responded, 'Jordan, how are you? What's happening? Where are you?'

'He laughed as he responded, 'I am fine. Lots happening and I am on Mylopotas beach on Ios.'

'Wow, the party beach.'

'I believe so, but I am not here to party. I followed Ms V here.'

'So you found her?'

Jordan realised that he needed to rewind the story. He informed Maria about how he had located Ms V in Filoti and tailed her to her place of abode in Halki village.

'Wow, that's amazing Jordan. Well done. How did you end up on Ios?'

'I just followed her here. It seemed like the right thing to do. I am glad I did though.'

'Why?'

He went on to explain how Ms V had deliberately searched for a girl on the ferry, imposed herself on the girl and then followed her to a beach resort on Mylopotas beach.

'That is very creepy Jordan.'

'I know. I am worried that something may happen to this girl.'

'So what are you going to do?'

'I don't know yet.' He went quiet for a few seconds. 'I don't think there is any point in involving the police at this point. It's probably best if I hang around and monitor things here for a while.'

'I agree. Why don't you go talk to the girl and tell her she may be in danger?'

'Because that would not be credible. She would probably think I was weird.'

'True. This is a hard one.'

'Leave it with me, Maria. I'll come up with something. Please don't mention anything to Mikalis.'

'I won't. Take care and let me know what you decide to do.'

'Will do. Yasas, filakia Maria.'

'Filakia.'

***

Maria was right, this was not an easy one. Jordan ordered another beer and decided to relax and try and let the solution come to him. As he sat back in his chair and looked out across the beautiful sandy beach and the glittering sea beyond, the girl appeared. She was with an older man who was showing her around the bar and its dining area.

He smiled to himself as he realised that the bar he was sitting in belonged to the beach resort, the girl had come here to work and she was obviously starting her first shift, the older man was probably her new manager. Jordan used his phone to check out the room rates of the nearby hotels, he could keep an eye on things very easily if he stayed close-by. There was a hotel next door with a vacancy and he booked it through an app on his phone. Before checking in to the hotel, he went off to buy some toiletries and a new T-shirt as he had basically arrived on Ios with nothing.

***

Athens

Vasilis arrived at the café in the busy Platia in Monastiraki and located his friend. Before he had even taken a seat, he asked the question. 'So, what did you find out?'

Dimitris replied. 'It's true, there are two missing girls.'

'I don't understand Dimitris. What has this got to do with me? Why do they want me to go to the Police, what purpose would that serve?'

'You tell me. It's all very strange.' Dimitris looked his friend in the eyes and asked him. 'Is there something I don't know, Vasilis?'

Vasilis said nothing in response, he just shook his head and shrugged his shoulders.

'So what are you going to do? What about this 24 hour ultimatum they have given you?'

'I think the best thing I can do is to get on that plane, head back to Melbourne and just forget this whole thing. I think this whole thing is some kind of extortion stunt.'

'But what about the missing girls and the threat to take another one?'

'Like I said, it's got fuck all to do with me. I came here to bury my daughter. The rest of this stuff is just bullshit I don't need.'

'So when will you head home?'

'The earliest available flight will be tomorrow evening. I'll see if I can get on that one.'

Ios

After settling into his room, Jordan returned to the bar where the new girl was working. He took a seat at the bar and started up a conversation with her at his earliest opportunity. 'Hi, I'm Jordan.'

'Andrea,' she promptly replied.

'Well it's nice to meet you Andrea. Have you worked here long?'

'I just started today,' she replied as she walked off to serve a couple sitting at a nearby table.

Andrea returned and asked the barman to prepare the drinks for the couple, as she waited, Jordan continued. 'Are you from Athens?'

'Yes,' she replied as she turned her head towards the barman.

Jordan was finding it hard to engage her in conversation, she was probably keen to impress her new employers, that was understandable. He decided to give her some space and moved from the bar to a table, as he stood to leave, he said. 'Excuse me, I can see you are busy. I hope your new job works out for you.'

She replied with a smile. 'Thank you.'

Jordan opened the picture of Katerina and Ms V, and made a copy of it. Then he cropped it so it just portrayed the face of Ms V. He set it as the wallpaper on his phone and displayed his phone face up next to his empty beer glass. He signalled Andrea and she approached his table. 'Could I have one more beer please?'

As she bent over to pick up the empty glass, she could not help but notice the image of Ms V and commented. 'How do you know that girl?'

'She is a friend, well, kind of. I met her on Naxos. It's a little embarrassing really. We got drunk together and I can't remember her name.' He looked at Andrea and she was smiling, his plan was working so far. 'I really liked her. She told me she was coming to Ios, so I came here hoping to bump into her.'

'You are not going to believe this, but she was sitting next to me on the ferry this morning. Her name is Vlora.'

Jordan sat up straight and feigned surprise. 'That's it, that's her name. I don't suppose you have her contact number, do you?'

'No, sorry. We only chatted. I liked her too.' Andrea smiled and continued. 'Ios is a small place, you may bump into her.'

'Hope so,' he replied.

Mergim leant over the handrail on the port side of the ferry, it had just departed Naxos and was heading for Ios. The warm evening air was gently blowing across his face as the sky darkened and the lights of the villages started to appear high up in the hills of Naxos.

Jordan decided to spend the evening in the bars that surrounded the scenic harbour of Ios. The hotel staff had advised him to avoid the Chora as it was renowned for its raucous night life and hordes of young party animals. The harbour was far enough away not to be troubled by them. He found a taverna and relaxed with an Ouzo and some grilled octopus, as he listened to the duo playing traditional Greek songs on guitar and bouzouki. His feelings were mixed, on one hand he was very relaxed due to the ambiance in the taverna and the surroundings, and on the other, he was concerned about Ms V and what she was up to. He would check up on Andrea tomorrow, but tonight he felt he deserved a few drinks and some great Greek food, he was slipping into tourist mode. The sun had dropped over the headland and performed its colourful exit long ago. It was approaching 11pm and the last ferry of the day was lining up to the pier. Jordan watched as the cars waited in line to board for the overnight voyage to Piraeus. The car headlights, bars and the ferry spotlights were combining to provide a unique scene. He captured some shots with his camera and while doing so, his attention was drawn to one particular car. There was something familiar about it. It was a blue Hyundai. He zoomed in to get a close up and picked out the driver and the red Olympiacos cap. Then he remembered why it was familiar, he had seen it and took a photo of it before, on Paros. He smiled and took another shot of it as it climbed the ramp and disappeared into the garage space on the ferry.

CHAPTER TEN

🜍

Monday 10th June

Ios

It was 10am and the sun was already warming the sand as Jordan jogged barefoot up to the small café at the north end of Mylopotas beach. It was the perfect spot to have breakfast. He was pleased with yesterday's efforts, he now knew the first name of Ms Vokshi, where she resided on Naxos, and that she appeared to be up to no good on Ios. What would today bring for him?

———

Athens

Vasilis rolled out of bed and walked over to the door of his room. He smiled with relief as he confirmed that there was no note posted under his door. The 24 hours had passed, by doing nothing he had obviously called their bluff and it had paid off. He had been successful in getting a seat on this evening's flight to Melbourne and would have the whole day to do some sightseeing around the outskirts of Athens. He showered and made his way down to the Hotel's parking garage. As he approached his hire car his stomach sank, as he read the words on the windscreen. *"WE WARNED YOU!"* He touched the windscreen, the words were written in blood. It was still tacky and it stained his fingers. He was panicking now. A few minutes earlier he had thought it was all over, now he was faced with this. He jumped in the car and turned the windscreen wipers on to wash the blood away. He thought about asking at the front desk to see if the hotel monitored the garage with CCTV, but decided not to. They may involve the police and he did not want to draw the wrong kind of attention to himself. His flight was this evening, he only had a few hours to kill then he could turn his back on all of this nonsense.

Ios

Jordan made his way back along the beach and headed to the resort where Andrea worked. He took a seat at the bar and ordered a coffee. The barman looked agitated and was muttering to himself as he prepared Jordan's drink. Andrea was nowhere in sight, Jordan asked the barman if she was working today.

'She is supposed to be here now,' came the angry reply.

Jordan jumped to the worst conclusion straight away and pressed the conversation with the irate barman. 'What time was she meant to start work?'

'She should have been here at 8am to lay the tables.'

It was approaching midday now and it was obvious that she was not just late.

'Maybe she paid a visit to the Chora last night and got lucky,' he joked with the barman.

'Well her room wasn't slept in, so maybe you are right.'

Jordan's concerns were consolidating into panic now. He took his coffee to a table furthest away from the bar and close to the roadside near the beach. He called Maria.

Maria answered, 'Jordan. Kalimera. How are you?'

Maria's voice was a comfort to him. He had missed her. 'Hi Maria. I am okay, but I think we have another situation here.'

'Go on, please.'

'The girl, the one that Ms V was following, has not turned up for work this morning.'

'No!'

'I managed to have a casual chat with her yesterday. Her name is Andrea. I used a little trick and got her to talk about our Ms V. By the way, I found out that her first name is Vlora.'

'Clever boy.'

'I am absolutely convinced this Vlora girl is involved in these disappearances now.'

'It's looking that way, isn't it? With another girl going missing, you don't need to be on Ios any longer.' Maria paused for a few seconds and said. 'Look, if I were you, I would ask no more questions. I think you need to leave the island straight away.'

'Yes, agreed. I am going to head back to Naxos and check out the property Ms V is using in Halki.'

'Just go Jordan, you don't need to be caught anywhere nearby.'

Athens

Vasilis drove down the coastal route from Athens to Voula. He would be able to lie low there for a while and pass some time until he needed to head to the airport. He left the hire car in a car park adjacent to Kavouri beach, then took a stroll along the beach. He had not noticed the car following him all the way from the hotel car park. He took a seat in a beach bar and called his friend Dimitris. 'The bastards have called again.'

'When? How?'

Vasilis explained how he had found the car. Dimitris detected his anxiety.

'Where are you now?'

'Sitting on the beach, south of Voula.'

'Okay. Stay calm. What time is your flight?'

'I have to get to the airport for 9pm this evening. My plan is to keep out of the way for a few hours, then go back to the hotel and pick up my things before getting the hell out of here and away from all of this crap.'

'Okay. Hang loose. I will meet up with you once you get to the airport so I can see you off.'

The conversation with his friend calmed him a little. He could always depend on Dimitris, he was a good man. Vasilis kept checking the time, it was dragging. He decided to go for a drive up to Mount Penteli, he had not been there since he was a kid and a visit to the tranquil countryside may help to calm his nerves. As he approached his car, he noticed the flat tire on the front driver's side. 'Malaka,' he called out loud. 'I suppose it will kill some more time,' he said to himself as he popped the boot to extract the spare tyre.

As he looked inside the boot he shouted, 'Fuck,' and slammed the boot closed as fast as he could. He looked around to see if anyone had heard him shout out. He was alone. His hands began to tremor involuntarily as he reflected on what he had just seen. It was the body of a female, she was bound and gagged and had a blood stained scarf placed around her neck. He looked around once more to make sure no one was looking and gently popped the boot. Vasilis slowly lifted it up and bent over to take another look at the captive girl. Her eyes were closed. He eased the scarf from her neck to look at the cause of the bleeding. There was no wound, only an L shaped mark, drawn on with some kind of pen. The blood had obviously been applied to the scarf, then placed around her neck. If she was dead, then this was not the cause. He reached over and touched her wrist to check for a pulse, as he did, her eyes opened and he witnessed her terror as she looked at him. Once again, he slammed the boot closed. His heart was pounding heavily in his chest and he was in full panic mode. He caught sight of a bus arriving on the main road running parallel to the car park, it was heading for Ellenikon, he would be able to connect with the subway to central Athens from that place. Without giving it anymore thought, he ran over and boarded the bus.

Vasilis reached Ellenikon and made his connection with the subway. By now he was realising what an idiot he had been. He had left a girl bound and gagged in a car hired in his name. She was conscious and had taken a look at him. He had to make it to the hotel and retrieve his passport and things, before the girl was discovered.

—◆—

Andrea had no recollection of how she was abducted. After completing her first shift at the bar, she had gone to her room and taken a long relaxing shower. Her last conscious memory was when she set the alarm on her phone for a 6:30am wake up. She wanted to take an early morning dip in the sea before starting work.

Mergim had entered her room half an hour before the end of her shift and lay under her bed. Thanks to a misspent youth in Albania, he had become skilled in the art of breaking and entry as well as pick pocketing and petty thievery, using his talent to target many an unfortunate tourist. He patiently waited for her to doze off and stealthily manoeuvred himself to stand above her while she slept. Within minutes, he had her bound and gagged. Then he arranged her bed to look as if she had not slept in it. The remainder of his task was easily executed, using the cover of darkness to place her in the boot of his car before catching the overnight sailing to Piraeus.

＿ww＿

As Andrea lay in the darkness of the boot, she replayed the scene she had visually captured in the short time the boot was opened. She had no idea who the man was, but he was clearly startled when she looked at him. She also picked up that she was in a car park and heard the sound of heavy traffic nearby. She wriggled over to make contact with the side panels of the boot interior and used all of her energy to make as much noise as she could by slamming her feet against the panels. It only took a few minutes for someone to respond. She heard banging on the boot, the acknowledgement of her cry for help. The voice of her rescuer, Mergim, was telling her to relax and that help was coming. He would be long gone before the police would arrive though.

———

Athens

Vasilis exited from the subway at Syntagma Square. He mingled alongside the many tourists that were already flocking to visit the Greek parliament building on the opposite side of the road to the subway stop. His hotel was situated on an adjacent side of the square and as he approached it, he stopped in his tracks as he saw the two police cars parked at the entrance. It was too much of a coincidence for him to discount the connection to his hire car and its cargo and the presence of the police at his hotel. He had been well and truly framed. He skirted around the opposite side of the square and made his way down Ermou Street, one of the main shopping areas of central Athens. He worked his way through the crowds of shoppers and located a barber shop. The change of appearance to short cropped hair and designer stubble would help him to stay undetected. It would certainly buy him some time to figure out how to deal with his situation. He was smart enough to know that his phone and bank cards would enable him to be more traceable, so he used them for the last time. He withdrew the maximum cash limit out at an ATM on all of his cards and made one final call to Dimitris.

'Listen carefully Dimitris, I am going to be quick. This has gone from bad to worse. Meet me at the café, where the road forks down to Thiseio on Apostolou Pavlou in an hour, buy a couple of mobile phones and bring them with you. If the police contact you, tell them that you think I have left the country already. Okay?'

Dimitris responded, 'Yes, will do.'

✤

CHAPTER ELEVEN

Monday10th June. Afternoon
Koufonisia

By the time Jordan arrived back on Naxos, news of Andrea's rescue in Voula had been circulated to the South Aegean Police. Mikalis used the opportunity to visit Maria and impress her with the latest developments. He made it sound like he had been personally involved.

Maria played dumb, she had to protect Jordan. 'So what did you find out about this girl? How was she abducted?'

'She couldn't tell us anything really. Apparently, she had been taken whilst she was sleeping. It looks like someone had managed to get into her room to take her. She had gone to bed on Ios and woke up in the boot of a car in Voula.'

'Goodness, how horrible. Was she hurt?'

'No, not at all. Apart from the trauma of being abducted. Strangely though, she had a mark on her throat. An L shaped one, someone had drawn it on with a marker pen.'

Maria's thoughts drifted back to Jordan's dream, the one about Katerina. Come tomorrow it would be two weeks since her friend had disappeared. So many thoughts were running around in her head. She was finding it hard to manage the conversation with Mikalis without accidently declaring what she and Jordan had found out for themselves. Now that Andrea had turned up alive, there was hope that Katerina and the other girl, Sophia, may be okay too. A thought came to her and she asked Mikalis. 'Have you checked Andrea's Facebook account?'

'How do you know her name is Andrea?'

Maria just stared back at Mikalis and said, 'I think you and I need to take a trip up to Naxos.'

―᷈᷈᷈―

Naxos

Jordan received the text from Maria. *"I will explain everything later. Mikalis and I are travelling to Naxos later today. Don't pursue Ms V before we get there. Meet us off the ferry. ETA 18:30. xx"*

Jordan replied. *"Do I need to be worried?"*

"No. xx."

This would be the first time that Jordan had set eyes on Mikalis since his enforced exile from Koufonisia. He was not particularly looking forward to meeting him, he did not trust him and didn't like him either. In truth, Jordan was jealous of Mikalis.

―᷈᷈᷈―

Athens

Dimitris walked from Thiseio Metro station and headed up the wide inclined pathway that provided a spectacular view of the Acropolis. His friend had obviously chosen a very popular and crowded tourist spot as cover from the police. Dimitris laughed out loud as he picked out his friends' new hairstyle and pulled up a chair next to him. 'Nice look, Vasilis. Now tell me, what the hell is going on?'

Vasilis looked around and lowered his voice. 'They've got me good and proper. I don't know what to do, Dimitris. They have planted the body of a girl in my car.'

Dimitris exclaimed. 'What! Was she dead?'

'No, but I thought so at first. It all happened so fast. At one point she opened her eyes and looked at me.'

Vasilis went on to explain how he had panicked and ran from the scene. How he had discovered the police at his hotel and was forced to abandon his passport and belongings. He deliberately omitted the fact that the girl had a mark on her throat and a bloodied scarf tied around it.

'This isn't good my friend.'

'Tell me something I don't know. What do I do, Dimitris?'

'It looks like they are holding all the cards. If I were you, I would try and make contact with them. You have to bring this to a close.'

'That's going to be easier said than done.'

'Sure. They have clearly boxed you into a corner for some reason. Wait it out, I am sure they will make the next move. They are obviously following you.'

As Dimitris uttered the words, Vasilis scanned the crowds around him and slouched back in his chair and quietly said. 'Okay you bastards, whoever you are. Bring it on.'

⸺⁓⸺

Naxos

During the journey to Naxos, Maria briefed Mikalis on what she and Jordan had learnt about Ms V. He listened intently then commented. 'Maria, you are treading on dangerous ground. This is a serious police matter and you are involving me on a personal level now.'

'Yes, I know that. But what other option do we have? You guys aren't getting anywhere fast with this. Besides we don't know for sure that this Vlora girl is directly involved. It's just very suspicious at this stage.'

'So what do you want me to do?'

'Help us put our minds at rest. Let us show and tell you what we've worked out so far.'

'This could get me in serious trouble, you know that?'

'I do and I am very grateful to you. You are off duty this evening and you will be back at work tomorrow morning. If there is any value in anything that we find out this evening, then you can make it look like you came across it and get the credit for it. How does that sound?'

He smiled and replied. 'Okay. By the way, cops are never off duty.'

The ferry turned into the harbour entrance for Naxos. The orange glow from the sun was illuminating the mass of white buildings that made up the beautiful Chora and its bustling water front restaurants.

Jordan watched apprehensively as the crowds of people poured onto the pier from the ferry. Maria spotted him and waved him over. He detected the look in her eye that suggested they play it cool in front of Mikalis, so he gently shook her hand and gave her a polite kiss on her cheek. He and Mikalis eyed each other as they exchanged a hand shake and Maria warned them. 'Now, you two. Play nice.' It had the desired affect and they all laughed.

Maria asked. 'Where to first, Jordan?'

'I've hired a car so we can take a trip up to Halki. We can update each other on developments on the way.'

Maria persuaded Mikalis to sit in the front alongside Jordan, she wanted them to try and bond. Jordan was both saddened and relieved to hear about what had happened to Andrea. At least she was safe and back home with her parents now. Mikalis was slowly building a respect for Jordan, his efforts to find Katerina and his concern for the other girls was admirable.

As they wound their way up to the mountain village, the sun was setting over the Island of Paros to the west. For most of the drive the sky was a mix of blood red and bright yellow, but the colours faded away as darkness set in as they slowed down and drove past Vlora's villa. Jordan parked up close to the centre of the village and turned his head towards Mikalis, inviting him to provide some direction.

'For what it's worth, I share your concerns about this Vlora girl. But we can't just go barging into her property. We have to be very careful that we don't spook her, she could go underground if we do.'

Jordan asked, 'Do you think there is any possibility that Katerina and the other girl may be in the villa?'

'It's definitely possible. Look, I think it will be best if I take a snoop around the property first.'

The trio walked down to the villa. Jordan noticed that Vlora's motor scooter was not there and informed Mikalis. The young cop advised them to take cover across the road from the villa and to text him if they heard anyone approaching. He crossed over the short picket fence and walked cautiously towards the front of the villa. All of the shutters were closed and he saw no sign of any internal lights through the glass panel above the old wooden front door. Access down the side of the property was only manageable from one side, the other was completely blocked with flora and dense under-growth. He edged his way down the side alley and stopped halfway to try and open a shutter, but it would not budge. As he reached the end of the alleyway, he turned into a courtyard at the rear. He could smell something burning. It was coming from an old 44 gallon drum, he walked over and peered inside. All that remain-ed was a few smouldering ashes.

Jordan was the first one to notice the car as it slowed down and pulled up in front of the villa. The male occupant got out of the vehicle and entered the property via the front gate.

Maria sent the text to Mikalis. *"Look out. Someone is coming in."*

Mikalis waited in silence as the second text arrived. *"He's gone inside."*

Jordan took a photograph of the car and its registra-tion plate as they waited for a reaction from Mikalis. A few seconds later they heard the sound of gravel being trampled as Mikalis emerged from the side alleyway. Just as he appeared in full view, the front door opened and the man stepped out. The men stared at each other for a moment and it was the visiting man that broke the silence. 'What are you doing on my property?'

Mikalis reached for his badge and held it up. 'Police.'

Jordan and Maria kept their cover and watched on as Mikalis stepped towards the man.

The man asked Mikalis, 'What do you want? Why are you here?'

'I need to talk to the woman that is staying here.'

'So do I.'

'Okay let's start again. Where is the woman that is staying here?' said Mikalis.

'I don't know.'

Mikalis was getting frustrated. 'Who are you and what is your business here then?'

'I am the owner. The woman was renting this villa from me. I got a text from her saying she was leaving. I've just looked inside, she's gone.'

Mikalis asked him. 'Could I take a look inside please?'

'Yes. But can I ask you why you are looking for her first?'

Mikalis did not want to venture into that discussion, so he asked the man. 'Are you declaring the rent she is paying you?'

The question clearly shook the man and he reacted with nothing more than a guilty smile.

Mikalis returned the smile. 'I would really like to take a look inside. Do you think that would be okay?'

As the man motioned towards the front door with his hand, Mikalis signalled to Maria and Jordan to come over and join them. As they crossed the road, Mikalis told the owner that they were with him.

Athens

Vasilis and Dimitris left the café and took the scenic route towards Monastiraki metro station.

'Look Dimitris. I am going to need somewhere to hang out. I can't go back to the hotel.'

'There's an apartment in Piraeus. It belongs to a friend of mine. He's away at sea for a few months. I always keep an eye on the place for him. You will be fine there.'

As Vasilis thanked his friend, they reached a busy street of restaurants. The path ahead of them was blocked with tourists and they pushed their way through the crowd. Dimitris noticed the frustrated look on his friends' face. 'Lighten up, it's good for the economy.'

Vasilis laughed. 'I suppose so.' He had felt the pressure on his side as he squeezed through the crowd and placed his hand in his pocket to make sure his cash and wallet were still there. They were. He slipped his hand into the back pocket of his jeans and felt something. He extracted it, it was an envelope. Vasilis stopped and called out. 'Hold on Dimitris.'

Vasilis turned to look back down the crowded street. Then he turned his attention back to the envelope and its contents as Dimitris looked on. It contained a ticket for a ferry. He was the named passenger and the booking was for Piraeus to Santorini, travelling on Friday 14th June at 7:30 am. Vasilis took another look down the street.

'They'll be long gone now, Vasilis. I told you they'd make the next move though, didn't I?' said Dimitris.

Naxos

The interior of the villa was dark, the heavy wallpaper and décor were reminiscent of something from the 1970's. There was a dank odour about the place. Mikalis asked the owner. 'How many bedrooms?'

He pointed down the central corridor. 'Three. They are at the back of the villa.'

'Did you light the fire?'

'What fire?'

'Someone has had a burn off in the courtyard.'

'Must have been her.'

Mikalis led the way to the bedrooms, as he opened the door to one of them, he asked. 'Was she staying here alone?'

'That was the arrangement. I didn't check though.'

Jordan and Maria watched as Mikalis performed a thorough search of the first two bedrooms. They reached the third room and the young policeman stopped at the door before entering. He bent over and touched the frame of the door, he turned his hand and looked at his fingers, they were showing traces of fresh paint.

Mikalis asked the owner. 'Could you wet a cloth and bring it to me please?'

The owner returned and Mikalis took the cloth and wiped over the section where he had detected the wet paint. It revealed two holes that had been filled and painted over. He moved his hand left and touched the door to discover more wet paint.

'This door has been padlocked.'

'Not by me,' said the owner.

Mikalis made no comment, he pushed the door open and they all entered. The room was devoid of a bed and furniture. 'Was this room always empty?'

'Yes.'

Maria touched Jordan on his arm and asked Mikalis. 'Are you thinking someone was held here?'

Once again Mikalis did not respond. He attempted to switch on the light and discovered that there was no light bulb in the holder. The owner walked into one of the other bedrooms and returned with a light bulb. With the aid of the light, Mikalis inspected the room. As he directed his attention to the wooden flooring, Maria walked over to the side wall and noticed some loose wallpaper just above the skirting. She pulled it away and uncovered the word, *"Help."*

Jordan called to Mikalis, 'Look at this.'

Mikalis dropped to his knees and took a closer look. He tugged at the paper and revealed the initials. *"K"* and *"S."* He ordered everyone out of the room. 'I'm going to call this in.' He turned to the owner and said. 'Sorry, but this villa is now a crime scene.'

―――

When Mikalis called his Sergeant, at first the conversation did not go well. But as the Sergeant calmed down and the realisation kicked in that this could be a good thing for both of their careers, it improved.

The Sergeant said, 'Secure the property and stick around until the detectives arrive in the morning, then get back here.'

Mikalis was feeling good about himself now, he smiled at Maria and replied to his boss. 'Yes Sir.'

Jordan and Maria wandered up to Halki village and left Mikalis and the owner to secure the villa. As they walked up the road, Maria reached over and took

Jordan by his hand and turned him to face her in the darkness. He was about to speak when she stood on her tip toes and kissed him passionately. It took him by surprise, but he responded immediately. 'I can't tell you how long I have waited for that,' he said.

Maria hugged him and replied. 'You are not alone there.'

Jordan pointed at the lights of a restaurant a short distance up the road and asked her, 'Should we?'

The air was still and the mood of the restaurant was just right for the occasion. Maria ordered a carafe of Rakomelo, a spiced raki drink served warm, and they toasted the hope that Katerina and Sophia may still be alive. Maria made a point of casually mentioning that she had booked a room in the Chora for the overnight stay. Her subtle hint that they would not be spending the night together pleased Jordan, he did not want to rush things anyway.

They had arranged to regroup with Mikalis in Naxos Chora in the morning, but the rest of the evening belonged to them.

Tuesday 11th June

Naxos

It was 8am and the Chora had not fully woken up yet. Restaurant staff worked at laying tables and washing the pathway that separated their kitchens to the long dining areas that sat adjacent to the beautiful harbour. Jordan selected the café with the best view of the port and harbour as he waited for Maria to join him. He could not be happier with the situation following yesterday's discoveries and also how his relationship was developing with Maria. His thoughts drifted to Mikalis and how the young cop had stepped up and managed the situation at the villa.

Maria pulled him away from his thoughts as she tapped him on the shoulder. 'Kalimera Jordan.'

'Hey, morning Maria. Did you sleep well?'

'Yes. My best one in a couple of weeks, thanks.'

Maria took a seat alongside Jordan and gently touched him on the hand. As she did so, she felt the presence of someone standing over her and assumed it was a waitress. She pulled her hand away sharply when she discovered that it was Mikalis. He gave her a look that confirmed he had noted the affectionate gesture. The atmosphere remained strained for a few minutes until Maria broke the silence.

'I couldn't believe how well you handled things yesterday, Mikalis. You were so clever.'

His response was tainted with an arrogance she had not witnessed before. 'It's my job.'

Jordan knew it was best for him to remain silent and observe their dialogue at this stage. Mikalis was obviously miffed at Maria's closeness to him.

'I know it's your job Mikalis. But I appreciate how you carried it out and would like you to know that,' said Maria.

He acknowledged her frankness with a respectful nod and offered to buy them all coffee.

'So what happens now? If I am allowed to ask,' said Maria.

'The Detectives own the investigation, they'll be calling the shots,' said Mikalis.

Maria asked him, 'Do you still have access to Sophia's Facebook page?'

'Yes, why?'

'I would just like to see her face again. Can Jordan and I take a look at her photos?'

Mikalis logged on to her page and handed his phone over to Maria. She flicked through the images and Jordan looked on. Jordan noticed something of interest on one of the images and asked Maria to go back to it. It was a photograph that had been taken from the rear seat of a taxi. He asked Maria. 'May I take a closer look?'

Maria checked with the stern looking Mikalis and handed the phone to Jordan. He expanded the photograph to zoom in on the dashboard of the taxi and revealed a red Olympiacos cap, the item that had drawn his attention. Then he slid his finger across the screen to move across the image and view the taxi driver identification card that was hanging to the right of the steering wheel. The image of the driver was clear and so was his name, Mergim Vokshi. Maria had been looking over his shoulder and she let out a gasp when she read the name.

Mikalis leaned over to take a look. 'What is it?'

'That cannot be a coincidence,' said Maria.

Jordan reached into his backpack and extracted his camera. 'It's not just the name.' He scrolled through his images and found the shots he had taken of the blue Hyundai, one on Paros and other on Ios. The image of the driver and his red cap were clear but had been taken from the side, as opposed to the identification card which was a front profile.

Maria asked Mikalis. 'Can you guys tell if that is the same person?'

Mikalis swallowed his pride and addressed Jordan directly. 'Could you send me those images? I will get them checked out.' Jordan nodded and Mikalis added, 'Good work.'

Maria cashed in on the moment and asked Mikalis. 'Does this mean Jordan can come back to Koufonisia?'

'Leave it with me. I will have to clear that with my Sergeant.'

A large blue ferry sounded its horn as it approached the pier. Maria responded first. 'That's ours. Come on Mikalis, we've got to run.'

Jordan waited until the young cop turned his back and sneaked a kiss on Maria's cheek.

As they crossed the road and ran towards the ferry she shouted. 'Thanks again, Jordan. We will be in touch.'

❧

CHAPTER TWELVE

Katerina's Abduction
Tuesday 28ᵗʰ May
Koufonisia

Katerina lay on her bed and watched as the morning sunlight adorned her room. She was loving Koufonisia and her new job as a waitress, working at a restaurant owned by a local family. The customers were great, mostly foreigners and they generally tipped well. The hours were demanding, but in spite of that she still managed to enjoy a fair amount of her free time with visits to the beach before her afternoon and evening shifts started. She had also made friends with another girl that was working the summer season, Maria. Maria worked in the travel agents on the main street that ran through the small but intensely picturesque Chora.

Katerina reached over to the dressing table next to her bed and picked up her diary. She read her last entry. It brought back the feeling of unease that she had felt on Pori beach. Today she was going to take the taxi boat over to the uninhabited island that lay a short distance south. It was named Kato Koufonisia. Everyone told her that it was an amazing place to spend a few hours of total relaxation, a genuine paradise. She slid out of bed and went to the bathroom to freshen up. Her favourite bikini was hanging off the shower head, it still felt damp so she left it there to dry and pulled on her second favourite one. Katerina checked the time and still had twenty minutes until the first taxi boat left. She hurried out of her apartment and skipped down the stairs and into the bakery below. It was nearly always the smell of the pastries and pies cooking below that woke her on a morning, as opposed to the sun shining in through her curtains. The girl behind the counter had already prepared her order of coffee and a spanakopita to go. No need for Katerina to wait in the queue with the tourists, she was classed as a local now and she made enough noise upstairs to let the assistant know she was on her way.

It was only a short walk to the departure point for the taxi boat. Katerina felt a warm feeling in her stomach as she admired the view of the pregnant lady island in the distance, Ammos beach in the foreground and the stretch of turquoise sea in-between, no one had to tell her how lucky she was, she knew it. When she reached the taxi boat there were already six passengers on board, some of them smiled at her as she stepped on. One more person joined just before the boat pulled away, a girl that appeared to be travelling alone. Katerina had developed an ear for the various languages spoken by the tourists. By the time the boat reached the halfway point to Kato Koufonisia, she had determined that she was travelling with visitors from Norway, France and Italy. The boat reached the top end of the island and went close into the shoreline, it sailed through the shallow water and seemed to hug the rocky cliffs only a few metres away. She saw many small bays and coves, some with Palm or Finika trees that would be ideal for natural shelter from the sun. The crew killed the boat engine and gently steered it towards a sandy beach. They skilfully manoeuvred the craft so it lay parallel to the beach, next to a sand bar that would allow the passengers to disembark with ease. She overheard a crewman telling the Italian couple that the boat would be at the same point for a pick up at 1pm. That would be ideal for her as she needed to be back on Ano Koufonisia for a 3pm start at the restaurant. It only took a few steps through knee deep water to reach the warm sand on the beach. Once there, she looked around for a good spot to lay out. It was too busy for her liking. There was a small pathway to the right-hand side of the beach, she figured it would lead to the shady cove with the Palm trees, that would be the ideal place for her. As she strolled along the pathway, she passed some nudists, fortunately her cove would be far enough away from them.

Katerina carried on until she reached a high point and looked down at three Palm trees that sat in a cluster a few metres back from the water's edge, the cove was tiny and private. She had found her ideal place. She settled into a spot under a tree and never noticed that the other single girl on the boat had followed her and was observing her from a distance.

There was a light breeze blowing, enough for the man on the dingy to move along at a good pace. She had noticed him during the crossing between the islands. Now he was just a short distance out to sea ahead of her cove. She rested back on her elbows and wriggled into the warm sand making sure her head was protected by the shade of the trees. For some reason, the image of a customer at her restaurant came into her thoughts. He was an Englishman, young and handsome. She had barely had any contact with him, but he definitely left an impression. As she lay back and closed her eyes, she smiled to herself, thinking of what this adventure may bring.

Vlora called her brother, explaining where the girl had settled. Mergim tacked his dinghy back and forth, never losing sight of the tiny cove with the palm trees. He edged the dinghy closer to the shore line on the left side of the cove. The dinghy came to rest on the beach, obscured from the cove by a rocky outcrop that extended into the sea.

Katerina was lying on her back and was wearing earphones. Everything looked good for an approach. As a medical student, Vlora knew how much Ketamine to administer. Vlora stepped into Katerina's footprints in the sand and scanned the surrounding landscape before taking the last few steps towards her. She threw the large beach towel over Katerina's face and upper body, then straddled her so she could inject the Ketamine into her thigh muscle. Vlora held her position for three minutes until Katerina's muffled protestations ceased and she stopped moving. Then she lay alongside her and waited. Mergim came into view first, he was in the water and was pulling the dinghy around the outcrop of rocks. Vlora gripped Katerina by the shoulders and gave her a shake, when she did not respond, she placed a vanity mirror over her mouth and watched as it misted up. Mergim lodged the dinghy in the sand and walked a short few steps to join his sister and their victim.

Things were going well, but the next action held the most risk, they had to get the girl into the dinghy in her unconscious state. It was not something they had planned in detail, as it was highly dependent on the situational circumstances that they would find themselves in. The location favoured them though. The cove was sheltered and only slightly overlooked, but only if there was some-one using the pathway behind them.

They eventually settled on a suggestion from Vlora. She would stand at the highest point of the pathway, the mound she had crossed earlier. Then she would pretend she was taking a photograph, whilst looking out for any-one coming towards them. Meanwhile, Mergim would pick up the girl in a fireman's lift and run to the sea and drop to his knees in the shallows, mimicking some kind of prank. From there he could lift her into the dinghy and place her in a seated position and quickly climb in alongside her.

They executed the plan to perfection. Vlora kept her station at the top of the mound until her brother had discretely repositioned the girl at his feet, bound and gagged her, covered her with a tarpaulin and pulled the dinghy well away from the cove. Her next task was to clean up the site where the snatch had taken place, then catch the 1pm taxi boat back to Ano Koufonisia.

Katerina had not stirred for the whole of the crossing. Using Ketamine was risky but Vlora had been cautious, the main objective was for the girl to remain unconscious until she was bound, gagged and out at sea on the dinghy. Mergim was closing in on the west coast of Ano Koufonisia. He had left his car parked off road, and within a few metres of the shingle beach of a secluded bay. The sailing dinghy had performed well and he felt a personal pride as he expertly brought it to rest on the beach. Before climbing out, he checked on Katerina, she was still out for the count. He popped the boot of his car and carried her over and gently placed her in it. He looked at her as she lay still and recalled how he had picked her up in the taxi a few weeks ago in Athens. Now she was here, captured as planned.

As Mergim drove off, Katerina started to come around. She began to panic, the motion, the darkness and the lack of ability to move her limbs were terrifying her. The effect of the Ketamine was also taking its toll. She had a blinding headache and felt nauseous. It also seemed to affect her memory, she was trying to recall her earlier movements and figure out how she got to be in the boot of a car. Her last recollection was leaving the bakery and heading down to catch the taxi boat.

Vlora and Mergim rendezvoused at the pier. They had timed events to perfection and had only 30 minutes to wait for their ferry trip to Naxos. Vlora parked behind Mergim and turned off the motor scooter engine and listened carefully. No sound was coming from the boot of his car, Mergim had made a good job of sound proofing it. She leaned over the front of the handlebars of her scooter and smiled into his rear view mirror, he acknowledged her message by reaching up and adjusting the mirror. There were two reasons that the car would not receive a spot check from the ferry crew, they had no time to do it and they did not see it as part of their duties.

The Vokshi's and their cargo arrived at the villa in Halki in less than three hours. Katerina was fully awake now, shivering with a combination of fear and the effect of the drug. She heard the sound of the boot mechanism click and only managed to catch a quick flash of light as Mergim simultaneously opened the boot and threw a towel over her face. Her captors were conversing in Albanian, she recognised the language, but had no idea what they were saying.

Katerina started to shake uncontrollably and Vlora placed a hand on her shoulder and said. 'Now now, take it easy.'

There was something familiar about the voice, but Katerina could not place it. It could have been anyone she had met over the past few weeks. The touch was gentle and calmed her somewhat, but did not allay her internal fears.

Mergim checked the surroundings, lifted the girl out of the boot and followed Vlora into the villa. He placed the girl on a chair at the kitchen table. With the face of the girl still covered, Vlora checked her vital signs and everything appeared to be fine. Vlora took a seat opposite Katerina and Mergim removed the towel to allow their captive to see them. Katerina took a few seconds to adjust to the light and set her focus on Vlora. She was still gagged so could not speak, but her eyes told the story. Vlora watched as Katerina's eyes widened in recognition of her. Vlora nodded to Mergim and he removed the tape from around Katerina's mouth.

Her eyes were full of tears as she addressed Vlora. 'I know you. We have met before.'

'Yes. On the ferry a few weeks ago.'

Mergim placed a small bottle of water and two aspirin in front of Katerina.

'Take them,' said Vlora.

'What are they?'

'It's only aspirin. It will help you get over the sedative we gave you.'

'What am I doing here, why have you done this to me?'

Vlora stared back at her without speaking. Katerina turned her head to look up at Mergim who was standing at her side. 'Who are you?'

Vlora responded. 'You don't need to know anything. You will be our guest for a few days. Just stay quiet and do as we tell you.'

Katerina started to cry and Vlora ordered Mergim to take her into a bedroom at the rear of the property. The room was in darkness, but the light from the passageway revealed a blow up mattress, a sheet and a pillow. He untied her bondage and left the room without speaking a word. She sat on the mattress and rested her back against the wall and tried hard to recall her meeting with Vlora on the ferry. The imagery was clear, Vlora had approached her and asked if she could take a seat at her table. Katerina remembered telling her about her summer job and how excited she was at the prospect of living and working on a beautiful island. But that was weeks ago, why had this girl come back into her life? Katerina hung her head in hands and prayed and prayed that the saints would rescue her.

Mergim had a smile from ear to ear as he stepped back into the kitchen.

Vlora looked up at him from her seated position at the table and held out a hand to receive a high five. 'That went really well,' she said.

'What happens now? Do we let her go?'

'No way. We need her for a while yet.' Vlora continued. 'Besides, she recognised me.'

Mergim was taking instruction from his sister and was happy to do so. She was younger but much smarter than him. 'Today was amazing, it gave me so much of a kick. Not just what we did together. I loved being on the open sea on the dinghy.'

'You're a good man Mergim. Don't worry, I need your help with plenty other things. Starting in the morning.'

Wednesday 29th May

Morning

It had been a terrible night for Katerina. She had not slept at all and had no idea of the time or where she was. Mergim removed the padlock and opened the door to her room. The light shining down the passage way hurt her eyes and she looked back into the darkness.

Vlora stepped forward and said. 'Time to freshen up, come with me.'

Katerina followed her to a bathroom. It was pretty dingy, an old green bath with matching shower cubicle, toilet and hand basin. The window above the bath had been boarded up from the inside. Vlora caught her looking at the window and smiled, then pointed to a change of clothing perched on a stool. 'Help yourself to those. You have ten minutes.'

Katerina heard the key turn in the lock from the outside, slipped off her second favourite bikini and soaked her weary bones in the warm shower.

Vlora tapped on the door and called out to Katerina. 'I'm opening it.'

Katerina was fully dressed and had the towel wrapped around her wet hair. Vlora motioned for her to follow her down the passageway and into the kitchen. Mergim was sitting at the table, which had been covered with a vinyl cloth. Katerina had no recognition of him as the taxi driver that her taken her to the port in Piraeus.

Vlora said, 'Now Katerina, just do as we say and you won't come to any harm. Understand?'

She did not understand, but nodded in agreement as if she did.

Vlora instructed her. 'Lie on the table, on your back.'

She sat on the table and swivelled around to take up a lying position. Vlora held her by the shoulders as Mergim tied tapes around her chest and legs.

'Okay, it's very important that you stay perfectly still,' said Vlora.

It was then that the involuntary shivers started. Vlora touched her on the hand and said, 'Relax, I told you we are not going to hurt you.' Then she turned to her brother and said. 'You won't have this problem when it comes to the real thing.'

For some strange reason, that seemed to have a calming effect on Katerina.

Vlora and Mergim reverted to speaking in Albanian. Vlora crossed over to a bench by the kitchen window and returned with a marker pen. She asked Mergim to hold Katerina's head still. Then she drew an L shape on her throat, starting to the left of the windpipe, moving down and crossing it and finishing on the opposite side just above the collar bone.

Katerina closed her eyes and started chanting a prayer under her breath. Vlora swapped the pen for a scalpel and gently placed it at the starting point of the line she had just made. Katerina flinched and sprung her eyes open as she felt the cold steel come into contact with her skin. Unable to move or react in anyway, she closed her eyes and continued with her silent chant. Vlora applied gentle pressure to the point of the blade and broke the skin then slowly moved it down the line for ten millimetres. She looked up at her brother and said. 'No more, no less. Okay.' He nodded and they changed positions. Now Mergim was in control of the scalpel. Vlora held Katerina's head and she watched as Mergim copied what he had just been taught, extending the incision by another ten millimetres at the same depth.

Vlora leaned over to speak into Katerina's ear. 'It's over. Now let's get you tidied up.'

Mergim was beaming, his sister had promised him a major role in things and now she had taught him some of her skills.

Vlora cleaned the wound they had just made and applied the sutures. 'Don't worry, this will heal nicely.'

Katerina was unimpressed with the unwelcome comforting words, she was just glad that she was still alive. Mergim untied her and helped her to take a sitting position at the table. She nervously stuttered, 'I don't understand. Why me? Please let me go home.'

Vlora responded to her. 'We can't do that. You are going to help us. There is something we have to do. Just go along with things and you will be okay.'

Katerina could not have been more confused. Her throat stung and she felt unsteady on her feet as Mergim led her back to the dark room. He waited until she positioned herself on the mattress before he closed the door and cut off the light from the passageway that illuminated her room.

✤

CHAPTER THIRTEEN

Emilia

Emilia was very beautiful, short blond hair and a slender figure, but she was not the princess that her family thought she was. She played the part well whilst she was in their company, but her private life was her private life, and she kept it that way. Her home life was a misery, brought on by her mother's obsessional hate for her philandering ex-husband, her father.

Everywhere she went she received an abundance of attention, but she was only interested in what came from the female gender. There was no place for boys in her life, it had always been that way. There were some very subtle hints about her sexuality embedded in her social media feeds, but she worked hard at not making her taste common knowledge. She craved the freedom that a job in the islands would bring, and that day came shortly after her eighteenth birthday.

Her mother and Uncle Manolis had taken her to the ferry terminal in Piraeus and had insisted on waiting until the big blue ferry pulled away before they left the coffee shack next to the ticket office. She watched and waved at them from the upper external passenger deck.

Piraeus faded into the distance and her new free life beckoned.

Wednesday 29th May, Midday
Amorgos

Mergim and Vlora had no part in tracking Emilia's passage to the islands, they already knew where she was. Their challenge was to isolate her so they could enact their deed.

Vlora prepared for her trip by dying her hair ash blonde and loading a backpack with essentials. Mergim would join her tomorrow. She left her brother to attend to Katerina at the villa before heading off to catch the afternoon ferry to Amorgos. Today was about locating Emilia, observing her, and setting the trap for tomorrow evening.

Katapola sits in a natural harbour and is one of three small settlements that greet visitors to the island of Amorgos. Vlora rolled her scooter down the ramp and motored along the waterside street of tavernas, restaurants and shops. It was her first visit here and she liked what she was seeing. As usual, she had done her homework and knew much about the tranquil island. Her first duty was to find the hotel where Emilia was working. It was 4pm and Vlora reckoned that Emilia, as a receptionist, would have at least another hour to work. She parked her motor scooter next to a café at the base of some steps and worked her way up through the narrow winding alleyways and sugar-cube houses until she reached the hotel. The view through the glass frontage of the hotel from the pathway allowed her a clear view of the lovely Emilia. Target confirmed, she walked further along the pathway and checked into the first available hotel with a vacancy. After throwing her luggage on the bed, she left the room and found a place to sit opposite the hotel where she could subtly monitor Emilia.

Naxos

Mergim's instructions from his sister were clear. Allow their captive two excursions to the bathroom and feed her twice. Vlora had no concerns in regard to her brother's behaviour towards Katerina, he was many things but not a sexual deviant, the girl would be safe. He was slightly obsessive, so she also knew that he would not miss the ferry to rendezvous with her on Amorgos tomorrow afternoon.

Amorgos

Emilia emerged from the hotel and turned right along the pathway to access the steps that led back down to the waterfront. Vlora followed closely and mounted her scooter when she reached the café. Emilia turned right onto the waterfront and stopped when she arrived at a bus stop. Vlora sat astride the scooter and watched. Emilia was dressed and made up for the evening. The bus arrived, it was the service to the east coast beach of

Agia Anna, via the Chora. Vlora tucked in behind it as it pulled away and made the steep climb out of the port area. As the road wound around and climbed towards the Chora, the views became more sensational. Several of the other Cyclades islands were visible, sitting magnificently in the Aegean Sea. The bus swung around into a tight Platia, this was obviously the drop off point for the Chora. Emilia stepped off the bus. Vlora parked the scooter and followed on foot. An orange light was engulfing the whole of the Chora, the sun was about to set and Emilia appeared keen to get somewhere to watch it go down. She settled for a rooftop bar, drew up a bar stool with views out over the west coast, and ordered an exotic cocktail. Vlora opted for a table some distance away, it was a perfect vantage point to observe her target at play.

The rooftop bar had begun to fill up with tourists looking to capture the sunset with their mobile phone cameras. The sun did not disappoint, vivid colours of red and orange contrasted with the brilliant blue of the evening sky to give them what they wanted. By now Emilia was on her third cocktail. She was flirting heavily with the waitress, touching her arm and even taking a photo of her. Vlora beckoned the waitress over, ordered a drink and asked her. 'Is she a friend of yours?'

'Not really, she is a regular here. But I wouldn't say she was a friend.'

'Sorry, it's just that she comes across as if you guys know each other. She is very familiar with you.'

The waitress leaned over and whispered in Vlora's ear. 'She likes the ladies I think.'

'Oh, that explains a lot,' Vlora replied with a smile as the waitress moved off to serve another guest.

It wasn't just the waitress that Emilia was showing interest in. She checked out every female that entered the bar, even if they were with male company. Vlora had established a way to progress, but it would have to wait until tomorrow evening. She finished off her drink and left the bar, being careful not to draw any attention from Emilia.

Naxos

Katerina was holding up well, considering her predicament. She was drawing on her faith for the strength to cope. Her mother had taught her to turn to the church in times of need. It had helped them to deal with the loss of Katerina's father when she was ten years old. She had watched her mother care for her sick husband for several years before his illness finally took him. She sat in the darkness and used visualisation to generate positive energy, creating mental images full of people and places that she loved. Her images gave her the light she was being denied. Once again, the Englishman who had visited the restaurant crept back into her conscious thoughts and she felt herself smiling at the thought of him. She reached out to her God and the universe and prayed that she would be returned to safety and the life that she loved.

Mergim crushed two sleeping pills and mixed them in with Katerina's food. It was 8pm when he knocked on the door and instructed her to use the bathroom then join him in the kitchen for something to eat. He was not concerned about her attempting to escape, it was not going to happen. As she stepped into the kitchen, he signalled for her to take a place at the table. The spiked meal was a bakery purchased moussaka. She knew she had to eat to keep her strength up, so she tucked in. He stared at her and eventually could hold his silence no longer. 'Are you okay?'

'What do you think?' she replied.

He did not respond, he walked over to the sink and slid his dinner plate into it. It was the first time Katerina had seen the back of his head. An image flashed in her mind. Seeing him from this position, combined with his accent and the tone of his voice, triggered her memory and she recalled him as the taxi driver that had picked her up in Athens.

As he turned back to face her, she said. 'I know you.'

His face remained expressionless as he sat back at the table and did not reply to her.

'Why me?'

He wanted to answer her, but the words of his sister were echoing in his ears. "Don't allow her to get close to you. She is here to serve a purpose. We have to be very careful."

Katerina detected a sympathetic look in his eyes and pressed him. 'You seemed like such a nice man when we chatted in the taxi. How has it come to this?'

He was struggling to stay immune from her understandable questioning. 'I am a good man. It's just that ....' He cut off when he realised that he was being sucked in. 'I have to take you back to your room now.'

Amorgos

Vlora was feeling pleased with her accomplishments. The night was young and she was in one of the most beautiful villages in Greece. The traditional Greek music and aromas of the food penetrated the air as she walked through the narrow streets of the Chora. She felt a sense of power and control, she was making things happen and was directing vengeance towards a person that needed to feel it. They were so close to executing a really important part of the plan. The reconnaissance mission was going well, Emilia had revealed so much in a public display of her private persona. No doubt there would be more to follow. Vlora reached a small Platia that hosted four tavernas. She picked one that gave her the best position to monitor events, ordered a well deserved beverage and silently toasted herself, her brother and the memory of her mother. The Chora only started to get really busy after 9pm, so Vlora relaxed with a few drinks and waited for the night life to kick in.

For some reason, the early season seemed to attract Scandinavian visitors, groups of girls especially, and Amorgos was a popular choice for them. Four Norwegian girls arrived in the taverna next to Vlora's. She watched them downing shots and enjoying the ambiance of the warm evening. They were in full party mode and it wasn't long before they moved on to find their next venue. Vlora was enjoying the street life so much that she almost missed Emilia passing through the Platia. On seeing her, she settled the bill and followed her up a side street. There were several lounge style bars on the street and Emilia drew up outside of the busiest one. Vlora kept her distance and looked on from a café on the opposite side of the street as Emilia unashamedly approached the Norwegian girls and asked if she could join their company. A couple of rounds of shots later and they were acting like old friends. Emilia wasted no time in singling out one of the girls for close attention. It took just over half an hour and Emilia made a move on the girl. Vlora crossed the street and entered the lounge bar, she wanted to make eye contact with Emilia. She arrived just in time to see Emilia follow the blonde haired Norwegian into the toilet area. The girl opened the door to the small female toilet. Emilia leaned over the girl's shoulder and whispered something into her ear. Then they entered the toilet together and closed the door.

When they re-emerged, Vlora seized the opportunity to make her connection with her target. She walked directly into her path, blocking her way between two tables. Vlora gave a prolonged smile to Emilia and looked deeply into her eyes, before standing aside to let her pass. Emilia looked slightly confused but the reaction was all that Vlora needed at this time. Vlora left the bar and stepped back onto the street. Emilia had sat back down with the girls, but she took a sly look over her shoulder at the departing Vlora.

<center>~~~</center>

Thursday 30th May

Naxos

It was 1am when Mergim quietly slipped the padlock off the hasp and entered Katerina's room. She did not stir when he stood over her and shone the torch light on her. The sleeping pills were obviously working. He walked over to the opposite side of the room, rested his back on the wall and slid down to settle in a seated position directly opposite her. Mergim turned the torch light off and sat in the dark room. The only sound was her shallow breathing. His senses were heightened and he felt every movement of the tear as it ran down from his eye and travelled over his right cheek, before falling from his face at his chin.

Amorgos

The intense heat of the Greek summer was still a few weeks away and the morning air had a freshness about it as Vlora stepped onto the pathway outside her hotel. She put on her sunglasses and pulled her floppy hat down to partially cover her face as she walked past the hotel where Emilia worked. Emilia was seated behind the reception desk, engrossed in her phone. There was no need for any contact with her until this evening and Vlora's main objective for the morning was to identify some secluded beach locations. The original plan was to remove her from the island in much the same way as they had taken Katerina, but the layout and geographical positioning of Amorgos made that very difficult. Everything would have to begin and end on Amorgos.

It was 9.30 am and the port was already a hive of activity. Vlora mounted her scooter and rode around the harbour to take breakfast in Ksylokeratidi, the settlement that looked onto the port and across the harbour to the open sea. She used the maps app on her phone to perform an aerial scan for coves and beaches worthy of a visit, and decided to venture to the coastal area close to the village of Lefkes. It took her 30 minutes to reach the village, it was nothing more than a few properties nestled in the hills south of Katapola. Several dirt track roads ran down to the coastline from the tiny settlement. The sandy coves at the end of the dirt tracks were ideal for her needs and, although navigation in the dark may prove tricky, the benefit of not being over-looked would be worth it.

Vlora rested her scooter on its stand and climbed onto a large rock by the road side. The wind was invigorating and along with the uninterrupted view of the southern Aegean Sea it combined to stir her emotions and fill her with a sense of pride. This evenings venture would trigger a predictable and unstoppable reaction, it felt good to be the person responsible for creating that.

Naxos

Katerina felt groggy and a little bilious when she was woken by the knock on the door. Mergim pushed it open gently to let the light penetrate the room to allow her a few seconds to adjust her eyes. She was blissfully unaware of his intrusion into the room during the night and although nothing happened, it was better for her that she did not know. Mergim invited her to use the bathroom while he prepared breakfast for her. She would be all alone in the villa until tomorrow and he allowed her some extra time outside of her confines as compensation. While she ate breakfast unaccompanied in the kitchen, he prepared the room, taking in a night light, bottled water and a bucket. All of the window shutters were closed and locked. There was no natural light in the villa and it gave the interior a gloomy and depressive feel. Katerina worked hard at blocking the negative emotions that the artificial light evoked. The villa also had a distinctive smell, the type found in houses that have not been lived in for a while. Her hearing had become more finely tuned, picking up on conversations between her captors and some external sounds. She had no idea where she was, but had deduced that she was not in a heavy traffic area. Two or three times a day she would hear the sound of a bus passing by, but it only seemed to be travelling in one direction.

Mergim entered the kitchen and Katerina resisted the temptation to speak. Her efforts to engage with him last evening had resulted in a quick return to the room. She felt that he was on the verge of opening up to her, but she was not going to push it, it was up to him.

He picked up her empty dishes and placed them in the sink, then turned back to face her. 'I need to take a look at your throat.'

Katerina did not reply. She tilted her head back as if to allow him permission.

Mergim gently eased back the gauze pad and in-spected the wound. His sister had told him to look for redness and any signs of pus. The wound was clear. He applied a fresh piece of gauze and asked her if she need-ed to use the bathroom again. She declined the offer and he led her back to the room. Her first action, once he closed and locked the door, was to turn off the light that he had placed in the room. She preferred the darkness.

It was approaching lunchtime when the tourist bus drove past the villa on its daily tour of the northern part of Naxos. Mergim patiently waited for it to pass and park further up the road before he stepped out of the villa and walked down the lane to retrieve his blue Hyundai car. There was more than an hour before the ferry departed Naxos for Amorgos. He would wait until he was onboard before texting his sister to let her know that he was on his way. He wound his way through the hills and descended down to the port. The roads were quiet, apart from a few tourists on quad bikes and motor scooters. Katerina was creeping into his thoughts and it disturbed him, there was no room for attachment to her. If Vlora knew what he was thinking she would be very angry with him. He consoled himself with the fact that he had refrained from having dialogue with her. It was close, but he was able to control his emotions and stopped himself from saying too much to her.

Amorgos

Vlora looked on from the port as the huge high-speed ferry made the turn into the welcoming harbour. It moved fast through the calm waters and only slowed to make the final turn to berth itself against the concrete wharf in Katapola. She waited for the cars to begin rolling down the ramp before she turned the key to start the engine on her motor scooter. The blue Hyundai edged towards her and she manoeuvred her machine to ride alongside it. Then she pulled ahead of it and Mergim followed her as they navigated through the crowds of passengers and stationary vehicles waiting to board the ferry for its return trip to Naxos, Paros and Piraeus.

Once they had cleared the port area and reached the open road leading to Lefkes, Vlora slowed down and pulled onto a grass verge. She parked up her scooter behind a dry stone wall and climbed into the car with her brother. 'How is everything at the villa?'

'Everything is fine. The girl is secured in the room and in good health.'

'Good. Drive on. I have found a perfect place, it's a small cove and out of sight too.'

They reached the track that led down to the cove. The loose stones and red dirt made the road difficult to navigate in the two wheel drive vehicle. Mergim raised his concerns. 'This will not be easy in the dark Vlora.'

'We will make it work Mergim. We don't have a lot of choice when it comes to venues.' The cove was within site and she pointed over to it. 'There it is.'

It was pointless to argue with his sister, she had made up her mind. This is the way it was going to be. They reached the end of the road and parked up. There was a channel of rocks between the road end and the sandy stretch of beach. The waves were creating a gentle lapping sound and an intermittent breeze stirred the leaves on the Finika trees that dressed the rear of the beach.

He asked her. 'Where do you want this to happen?'

'To the right, under the tree.'

Mergim set to work, laying the tarpaulin and covering it entirely with a few centimetres of sand. He placed a few rocks on top to mark out the perimeter of the concealed tarpaulin. Vlora looked on and nodded her approval at his handy work. 'Now. Let's head back up.'

Mergim fitted a device to the toe bar of the car. It was a series of chains, designed to drag over the road surface and remove the tyre marks he was making. Vlora watched as he pulled away and drove a few metres up the track. She jumped back in the vehicle with him and said. 'Good job. Not perfect, but it's good enough.'

The car laboured slightly as it climbed out of the cove, but recovered its power when the road levelled out and zig zagged its way towards the settlement at the top.

Vlora gave her brother an update on her discoveries from last night and outlined the plan for this evening. He sniggered at her strategy to entice Emilia and it drew an angry response from her. 'Look. We have to do what we have to do to make this work. Just make sure you don't give the game away. We are only going to get one shot at this. Got it?'

He looked sheepishly at her. 'Yes Vlora. I won't let you down.'

They reached the point where she had left her scooter, and as she exited the car she said, 'Wait for my call. But it won't be before 9pm.'

Emilia was putting the last touches to her make up when Vlora entered the hotel reception. She immediately recognised her as the girl that had stepped in her way and gave her the eye last night. She put on her best smile and welcomed her. 'Yasas.'

Vlora responded in English. 'I am looking for a room for this evening. Do you have anything available?' Vlora knew that the hotel was fully booked as she had checked online already.

Emilia provided the inevitable response. 'I am sorry, we are fully booked tonight.'

Vlora put on a disappointed look and said, 'Okay. That's a shame. I liked the look of this place.' She spun around and walked towards the exit, paused, then turned back to face Emilia. 'Where do I know you from?'

'I think you may have seen me in the Chora last night.'

Vlora faked her response and deliberately ran her fingers through her soft ash blonde locks. 'Yes. I remember now. It's such a beautiful place, isn't it? Perfect for sundowners.'

Emilia replied. 'I love it.'

Vlora put on her seductive smile and said. 'I am heading up there tonight. Would you like to join me for a drink?'

'That would be great. What time did you have in mind?'

'There's a rooftop bar just a few metres up from the Platia. Probably the best place for a sundowner. How about 6.30 pm?'

'Perfect. I know that place well.'

Vlora smiled and said, 'It's a date then,' as she stepped out of the hotel.

She turned right as if to walk back down to the port area and heard Emilia calling to her from the front doorway. 'There is a nice hotel a few places along to the left of us. You may want to try that for somewhere to stay.'

'Oh, thank you. Sorry, I didn't get your name.'

'Emilia. My name is Emilia.'

The risks were evident to Vlora. It was a small island, and although the locals missed nothing when it came to comings and goings around them, they were not generally on the lookout for serious crime. She had more chance of being picked up by watchful eyes if she was a pickpocket. Island councils were well aware of the detrimental effect of petty crime, and much of the focus for policing was based on keeping that controlled and contained. So, all in all, she felt that she was able to move around without drawing much attention to herself.

Vlora arrived at the rooftop bar and paused at the top of the stairway to see if the waitress from last night was working. She wasn't, so there would be no complications there. Emilia was already sitting at the bar. Vlora approached her and gently placed her hands over Emilia's eyes and whispered in her ear. 'Guess who?'

Emilia spun around on the bar stool and instinctively pecked Vlora on her cheek. Vlora was delighted, the greeting could not have been more appropriate and it aligned with her vision for the direction that the evenings events should take.

'I took a chance and ordered you an Aperol Spritzer.'

'Wow. You must have sixth sense,' said Vlora.

The girls chinked glasses and stared out from their elevated position to the sensational vista that spread out before them.

Vlora's plan was simple. Lead Emilia on with some sexual provocation, get her intoxicated and invite her to the secluded beach for some girly fun. Emilia took no encouraging. She was well up for a liaison with the pretty stranger. When darkness set in and Vlora suggested calling a cab to take them to a private spot for some intimacy, she jumped at it.

Mergim received the message from his sister and waited patiently at the Platia for them to arrive. Emilia was too far gone to question if the taxi was genuine or not, she clambered into the back seat with Vlora and snuggled in to hug her latest conquest. This was Mergim's first visual of Emilia. He had seen photographs of her, but seeing her close up in the flesh excited him. He went through the motions of asking Vlora where she wanted to go and drove off towards the sandy cove.

Emilia's last drink in the Chora was spiked with a sedative and her consciousness was beginning to falter. She kept asking Vlora the same questions over and over. 'What's your name again? Where did we meet?'

Vlora let her ramble on without answering. They were about to reach the cove and in a couple of minutes Emilia would pass out.

The moonlight was strong and Mergim navigated the track without lights. As they reached the end of the track, Emilia muttered something incoherent and closed her eyes. Mergim stepped out of the car and walked over to the rocks and looked back up the steep hill that they had just driven down. They were completely alone and the only sound was coming from the waves as they poured over the sand on the tiny cove.

Vlora checked for a pulse on Emilia's neck, it was faint and her breathing was shallow. Mergim opened the rear door and lifted Emilia out and over to the spot under the tree that had been prepared earlier.

Vlora used the light from her torch to illuminate the area around Emilia's throat. She looked at her brother and asked him. 'Are you sure you can do this?'

'Yes I am. You promised.'

'Okay, go gently.'

Mergim leaned over Emilia, he visualised an L-shape and placed the scalpel at the starting point. He pressed gently and broke the skin. Emilia moaned lightly and he stopped and looked at Vlora.

She encouraged him, 'It's okay. Keep going.'

He placed the edge of the scalpel to pick up where he had left off. The blood flow was slight and Vlora mopped at it as Mergim moved slowly down and across Emilia's throat.

Vlora's tone was assertive. 'Finish it.'

Mergim raised his head to look at his sister. At that precise moment, Emilia convulsed, thrusting her head upwards and spewed green bile onto her chest. There was nothing they could do to counter the violent movement. When they set their eyes back on her throat, they saw the dark stream of blood flowing from her artery.

Vlora reacted first. 'Shit. Shit. Shit.'

'What is it Vlora?'

'Get that tarpaulin from under her and let's get out of here.'

Mergim was trying to comprehend what had just happened.

Vlora shouted. 'Fucking now, Mergim.'

Emilia was bleeding out. It wasn't a clean cut through her artery, but the nick was enough to be fatal, without any precise medical attention.

Her body gently rocked from one side to another as Mergim retracted the ground sheet that lay under her. It left a clean flat impression in the sand around her, erasing any sign that Vlora and Mergim had been there. As they departed the scene, they were careful to use the rocks for their passage back to the car. Once again, Mergim set the chains on the toe bar.

Before they climbed into the car Mergim asked his sister. 'Can't we save her?'

'We didn't come here to save her Mergim.'

'We didn't bring her here to kill her either,' he replied.

'Just go now,' came the order.

It took Emilia a bit longer than normal to bleed out and die due to her semi-comatose state. She would not regain consciousness at any point. She was discovered by chance by a man that had gone to the cove to do some early morning beach fishing. His vehicle and foot-fall had done a good job of eliminating any residual evidence left over by Vlora and Mergim. By the time the authorities were alerted, the Vokshi's were a few nauti-cal miles away from the port off Naxos, after escaping on the morning ferry from Katapola.

Emilia was not meant to die. She was supposed to be found alive on a secluded beach with a very distinctive wound on her neck. The intent was to force her estranged father to return to Greece. Once he recognised the characteristics of the wound and where the attack occurred, part two of the plan could be enacted. Her death was regrettable, but it guaranteed his return to Greece for her funeral.

Friday 31st May, Midday

Naxos

Katerina heard them return and enter the villa. They were arguing in Albanian, but it was clear that Vlora was very angry with her brother. Doors were being slammed and there was also the unmistakable sound of a glass being smashed. There was more shouting from Vlora, then Katerina heard her say in Greek. 'See to her.'

Katerina heard the sound of the lock being removed and the door pushed open to reveal a sheepish looking Mergim. He said. 'Please,' and motioned for her to use the bathroom.

Something had obviously gone wrong and Katerina hoped that it would work in her favour rather than against it.

☿

CHAPTER FOURTEEN

Sophia's Abduction
2nd to the 5th June

The decision to take another girl was not part of the original plan, but Emilia's death had changed everything. The police were now involved at a more intense level and the Vokshi's needed to give themselves space to operate more freely. One murder and two abductions would stretch the police resources heavily and provide an additional layer of panic to the authorities that were desperate to keep everything looking normal and safe.

When Mergim picked up Sophia in his taxi to take her to the port, he gleaned as much information from her as he could. Which island she was going to, her new place of employment, and as much about her personal life as she was prepared to divulge. Once he dropped her at the port in Piraeus, he sent images, videos and information about her to his sister. Vlora was waiting nearby and purchased a ticket for the same destination, she boarded the ferry and casually made acquaintance with the girl. It was the same methodology that they used for Katerina weeks earlier.

The next step for Vlora was to lose herself in the crowd as they disembarked from the ferry and then discretely follow Sophia to identify opportunities for an abduction. It amazed Vlora at just how easy that was. People gave so much away about themselves without realising it, especially young naive girls that wanted to trust others and fit in to lifestyles that they had fantasised about. Daily habits and preferences for recreation were key indicators for tracking someone.

The girl would have to be separated from the pack and that was much more likely to happen on a remote beach or in their place of residence. Sophia had already told Mergim that she would be exploring the beautiful beaches of Antiparos on her time off. Those beaches happened to be very accessible by small craft, and a sailing dingy was the ideal choice for anyone wishing to make a relatively quiet approach to them.

Sophia was totally oblivious to the fact that she had been under surveillance for a couple of days. Nor had she any reason to suspect that the man on the dinghy out at sea and the girl lurking in the trees behind her would take her while she slept on the warm sand of the tiny bay.

The take went without a hitch, there was not a sole in sight as Sophia was covered with a towel and sedated. However, complications arose in regard to taking her back to Paros on the dinghy. As the Vokshi's looked back towards Paros and the village of Pounda, which lay directly opposite them, a large amount of kite-surfers had taken to the air. The chance of detection was too high and Vlora demanded that Mergim hold the girl on Antiparos until the coast was clear.

The location of the cave was fortuitous. Its entrance was only visible from the sea and Mergim had noticed it whilst he was making his final approach in the dinghy. It was an ideal place to lay low and detain the girl. Once Sophia was moved to the cave, bound, and gagged, Vlora left the scene. Mergim would manage Sophia's transfer in the morning and Vlora would meet up with him again at the Villa in Halki on Naxos.

<hr />

Thursday 6th June, Morning

Naxos

When Sophia regained full consciousness, she went straight into a panic attack. She was in a dark room and that was all she knew. Her memory was fuzzy and she felt sick. She started to hyperventilate and jerked as someone placed an arm around her.

Katerina tried to calm her. 'Take some deep breaths. Slowly, slowly. You are not alone, I am with you. I am Katerina.'

'Where am I? What has happened to me? Why am I here?

Katerina calmly asked her. 'What's your name?'

'Sophia.'

'Some people have taken us, Sophia. I don't know why.' Katerina hugged her. 'Just try and calm down.'

As Katerina tried to comfort Sophia, she heard the sound of the lock being removed from the door. Vlora entered the room and allowed the light from the passageway to illuminate the space so she could look at the girls. She had been listening outside for a while and was aware of Sophia's anxiety. It was the first time that Sophia had set eyes on Vlora since the abduction, and she recognised her instantly as the girl that had app-roached her on the ferry only a few days before. She was too worried to speak and edged closer to Katerina.

Vlora broke the silence. 'Oh, you recognise me?'

Sophia responded with a slight nod of her head.

'Listen. For your own sake, go along with what we tell you to do.'

Vlora let the girls out one at a time to use the bathroom. She was concerned about Sophia's state of mind and nervous disposition. Although she was of similar age to Katerina, there was a huge difference in their maturity. Vlora made her mind up that Sophia would be the first one to be offloaded when the time came.

✿

CHAPTER FIFTEEN

Wednesday 12th June. Morning
Palaio Faliro, Athens

Vasilis slid the door open and stepped out onto the balcony. The hideaway place arranged by Dimitris was on the third floor of an apartment block, situated in the upmarket suburb of Palaio Faliro. It overlooked the busy coastal road, and from its elevated position it had unspoiled views of the sea and the islands closest to Athens.

As he drank his morning coffee, he stared out at the island of Aegina and the glistening sea that surrounded it. He had tossed and turned with his thoughts all through the night. He wanted to strike back at whoever was targeting him, but he had no idea who that was. However, he believed he knew why. The scar on his dead daughter's neck and the demand to meet him in Santorini was enough of a clue for him. He was desperate to take the offensive and break out of the trap he was in. It was 8am and several ferries were departing for the Cyclades Islands, he watched them as they set their courses in the shipping lanes as they left the port.

The thought occurred to him that every move he was making was reactive. They were pulling his strings at every turn and that was the first thing that he had to change.

Cancelling the trip to Santorini altogether was not an option. There would be no closure or escape for him until he faced them and they obviously wanted that to happen on Santorini. He decided not to take the ferry on Friday, as they had demanded. It would be so easy for them to set him up again with the police, should that be their plan. He would travel today using a different route. He was also concerned that they may already know where he was hiding out, so he had to come up with a plan to leave the apartment incognito, as soon as possible.

Vasilis stepped back inside the apartment and searched through the belongings of the absent owner. He selected a change of clothing and a baseball cap. He found a set of keys hanging in the entrance hallway. The motif on the key fob informed him that Dimitri's sea faring friend was the owner of a Vespa motor scooter. The key also had a remote control attached, probably for a garage door. He gathered his things and headed out of the apartment and took the internal staircase all the way down until he reached a door at the bottom, he pushed it open and there sat the Vespa in the basement garage. Vasilis triggered the remote and the garage door opened, he pulled the baseball cap down as far as he could and gunned the Vespa up the incline and out onto the coast road. He smiled to himself and he was sure that no one had witnessed his departure.

Naxos

It was always Vlora's plan to desert the villa in Halki. The timing for the exit was more good luck than good management though, and she had no idea of the events that occurred at the villa following their departure. By the time Mikalis and the others were making their discoveries, the Vokshi's and their cargo were settling into a vacant holiday home in Kastraki, halfway down the west coast of Naxos. Mergim had found the venue a few days earlier, and by courtesy of a local tavern owner, had ascertained that the British owners would not be using the property until late July. The three bed-roomed villa was set back off the main road and was accessed by a private gravel track. Forcing an entry was an easy job for Mergim, there was no security system and the trusting owners had actually left a window ajar at the rear of the property. They had also kindly left spare sets of house keys hanging on a home sweet home key board just inside the front doorway. The theft of a white panel van was also a bread and butter task for him. He doctored the registration plates and stored the van out of sight at the rear of the villa.

Vlora was delighted with her brother's unlawful skillsets, but she had other concerns about him. She had witnessed the way he looked and interacted with Katerina. It was obvious that he had feelings for her. There was no way that those feelings could be allowed to develop. In many ways Katerina had served her purpose and was becoming surplus to requirements as each day passed.

When word reached Vlora that Vasilis had made his premature departure from the apartment, it left her with a critical choice to make. On one hand, she would be delighted to get rid of Sophia, the girl was a liability. The only problem with offloading Sophia was that she may talk. On the other hand, Mergim's behaviour towards Katerina also posed a risk. It was down to her alone to make the call and she decided that Sophia would be the one to go first, but only after a conversation with her.

Vlora took Sophia aside and out of earshot of Katerina. 'You see Sophia, we know where your mother lives and we will find out quickly if you talk to the police, or anyone for that matter.' Vlora touched her on the lips. 'So you best keep this shut if you know what is best for you. And your mother.'

—⁓—

Midday

Naxos

It was only 24 hours since Jordan had said goodbye to Maria on Naxos, but he was missing her desperately. He so much wanted to be able to return to Koufonisia and was waiting patiently for word back from the young cop, Mikalis. He texted Maria.

"Kalimera Maria. Have you heard anything from Mikalis?"

She responded with a phone call. 'Hi Jordan. I thought it would be best to call you. How are you?'

'Fine, but missing you.'

'You are too sweet. I miss you too.'

'So, can I come back to Koufonisia?'

'Not yet, apparently the Sergeant does not think it's a good idea, he says it's a challenge to his authority.'

Jordan fell silent, he had hoped that Mikalis would push the case for him to return.

Unbeknown to Maria, Mikalis had not even discussed it with his Sergeant, he was determined to control the situation. Jordan was a source of help to him and that was all. There was no way that he was going to aid the relationship between Maria and the Englishman.

Maria picked up on Jordan's silence and said. 'Don't be too disappointed. We will find a way to be together.'

'Okay. Let's work on that then.' He changed the subject. 'What about the photos that I sent to Mikalis? Have the cops been able to identify and trace the Vokshi's?'

'Mikalis said not. Vokshi is a very common name in Albania and it is very likely that they crossed the border illegally. The taxi driver's identification card was a fake. Mergim Vokshi is not a registered taxi driver.'

'And the blue Hyundai?'

'They found it burnt out in southern Naxos.'

'So they could be anywhere from the mainland to Crete?

'Looks like it.'

'So what do we do now Maria?'

'Stay where you are for now, Jordan. I'll try and get some time off to come and see you. Yasas, Filakia.'

Jordan relaxed back into the soft cushioned seat at the front of the cafe and looked out at the eclectic mix of boats in the harbour. He was disappointed at not being granted a return to Koufonisia. But maybe it was a good thing, there was little chance that the Vokshi's would be going back there, he could be more useful where he was. It was approaching lunchtime and the crowds were starting to populate the many harbour side restaurants. He ordered another coffee and watched as several taxis drove past on their way to drop tourists off at the two huge ferries that were berthed on the pier.

He was too slow to react with his camera when he saw the man in the red Olympiacos cap drive by in a white panel van. Jordan's heart skipped a beat when he recognised the driver as the man he now knew as Mergim Vokshi. He stood up to run after it and was called back by the waitress to pay the bill. The last thing he wanted was to be arrested for doing a runner over a couple of coffees. He could only look on at a distance as the van joined the queue to board one of the two ferries. He thought about calling Maria and telling her to inform Mikalis, then decided not to. He did not have any credible evidence to offer and certainly did not want to send Mikalis's Sergeant on a wild goose chase. He would have to keep this one to himself for now.

Jordan was in a reflective mood. He flicked through the images on his camera and collected his thoughts on the happenings of the previous couple of weeks. So much had happened and events were having a massive impact on his life. It all started with a strange dream in a hotel room and now he was exiled on an island and love sick for a girl he barely knew. He caressed his camera and considered what his next move should be. The thought of just sitting and waiting for something to happen was irritating him. It occurred to him that he had done all that he possibly could in respect of Katerina's disappearance. It was up to the Greek author-ities to finish the job now and why should it be up to him to better the career prospects of an egotistical police sergeant and his rookie sidekick? He walked over to a ticket office and looked at the ferry departure board situated at the entrance. It was time to move on. He had to choose from the list of islands and the answer lay in his hands, his camera. Santorini was the wedding capital of the Greek islands and the obvious choice for him to earn some decent income and to move on with his life at the same time. It didn't matter where he located himself, if Maria wanted to be with him, she could just as easily travel to Santorini to see him. His mind was made up, he stepped into the office and purchased a ticket to travel on Thursday afternoon. His mood shifted to one of elation at the prospect of moving on and he decided to celebrate with an ouzo and some Greek snacks at his favourite restaurant. After placing his order he texted Maria. *"I am leaving for Santorini on Thursday."*

Within seconds of the message being delivered his phone rang, it was Maria. 'This is spooky.'

Jordan laughed and responded. 'What is?'

'That you are going to Santorini. I have just quit my job. I am going there on Friday to look for a new one.'

Maria explained that she had reflected on the conversation with him and that staying on Koufonisia was no longer an option for her. There was no point, it was only a job after all.

'This is amazing news Maria. We have done all we can to help the cops and all we get is strife from them.'

'Exactly. It's time for us to think about ourselves.'

'Have you told Mikalis about your plans?'

'No. I owe that Malaka nothing. He is all about himself.'

'And Katerina? How do you feel about stepping away from our search for her?'

'What more can we do Jordan?'

Jordan considered telling Maria about his sighting of Mergim and thought better of it. If they were truly going to move on, he had to step away and draw a line under it. His conscience was clear.

'Text me to let me know what ferry you are taking to Santorini and I will meet you at the port on Friday.'

'I can't wait,' said Maria as she hung up.

The intake of food and alcohol had made him feel tired and the lack of breeze at the restaurant added to his restlessness. Agia Anna beach was a short walk away and he knew there would be a welcome breeze coming off the sea, a sunbed and the shade of an umbrella was exactly what he needed.

The beach was busy but not over populated, in a few weeks time it would be impossible to find some personal space, let alone a vacant sunbed at this time in the afternoon. He watched as young mothers entertained their small children in the shallow waters of the sheltered bay. This would be his last night on Naxos and he would have to return the hired motorbike prior to boarding the ferry tomorrow afternoon. As he dozed off, he pictured himself taking a sunset ride down the coast to cap off his stay on what was one of his favourite places.

Palaio Faliro

Within eight hours of Vasilis making his escape on the Vespa, the Athens police were attending the scene at the apartment in Palaio Faliro to rescue the terrified young girl. She told them nothing, she just cried uncontrollably and told them that she wanted her mother. They decided to let her settle for a couple of days, they intended to try and talk to her again when she was less traumatised. However, time would make no difference to Sophia, she would never reveal anything about her horrific experience. She had no reason to doubt Vlora's threats. Her trip to paradise had become a living nightmare and she wanted to forget every minute of it.

The police collected and bagged the clothing that Vasilis had discarded on the bed. It would provide an abundance of DNA and would eventually match up with that which they found in the Athens hotel room that he had deserted a few days earlier. He was their main suspect in regard to the abductions. The Vokshi's were also of interest to them, but on a lesser scale. A couple of photographs posted on a social media site and some coincidental sightings of them were very poor forms of evidence. Even the scribblings on the wall of the villa rented in Halki by Vlora meant nothing without corroboration from Sophia. The detectives worked on the theory that the abductions by Vasilis Kostas were based on some kind of revenge mission associated with the death of his daughter. The only conflicting issue was that the missing girl from Koufonisia, Katerina, seemed to have disappeared prior to Emilia's murder. But in light of the fact that two abducted girls had now shown up, it was becoming more probable that Katerina may not be linked to the case at all.

Southern Aegean

Vasilis leaned against the railings on the stern of the ferry. He barely resembled the person pictured in his passport. He was oblivious to the fact that Sophia had been planted in the apartment and also blissfully unaware that an undercover police officer had just walked past him. The police had increased their presence on the ferry services to the islands in response to the murder and abductions, but it was little more than a token effort. In truth, the authorities were putting more effort into damage limitation than they were into finding the perpetrators. They believed that the worst was over and that the problem would soon go away.

Vasilis's ferry was bound for Mykonos, he figured the party island would be the best place to lay low for a while before connecting to Santorini on Thursday.

After disembarking from the vessel, he walked over to the crowd of hoteliers waiting by the taxi rank at the port. As he closed in on them, they lifted and waved the boards bearing their hotel names as they competed for his attention. It was the third one that he spoke with that got his business. He liked the sound of the accommodation and the fact that they would transport him there. It was no more than a bedsit above a supermarket, but it was cheap and a cash only deal.

They arrived at the destination and Vasilis felt the phone buzzing in his pocket, it could only be one person and he decided to ignore the call until he was alone. The hotel owner showed him up to the tired looking room and smiled as he gave him the key and held his hand out for the cash.

Vasilis waited for the landlord to leave and then he called Dimitris, 'Sorry, I couldn't take your call before.'

'Where the fuck are you?'

'I decided to leave early. I've had a gut full of dancing to their tune. I need to start calling a few shots.'

'What's fucking going on at the apartment? I can't get near it for the cops.'

Vasilis was totally confused, 'What? I have no idea what you are talking about Dimitris.'

Dimitris pressed his friend, 'Where are you?'

Vasilis stalled, 'I'm keeping that to myself for now.'

'Why?'

'Because I have no fucking clue what is going on.' He held the phone to his forehead for a few seconds before continuing. 'Find out what's happened at the apartment and call me back when you have something to tell me.' Then he cut the call.

It was not so much that he distrusted Dimitris, his friend had been solid and was there for him, he just needed time to think. His head was spinning. He looked at the phone, then pulled the back off it and removed the sim card. Whatever was going on at the apartment could have no bearing on how he was going to move forward, he could not let that influence his decision making. He was going to take the offensive and was not going to share that with anyone, including Dimitris.

The room was dingy and stank of mothballs, he needed fresh air and some space to think. He was on a main road in Platos Gialos, close to one of the most cramped and expensive beaches in the Cyclades Islands. He hated Mykonos, but he would be less conspicuous there than some of the other family orientated islands. With a little imagination, he would blend in nicely with the party crowds that embraced every gender and age group. He reached the bottom of the road, close to the beach entrance, went into a supermarket and purchased a half bottle of raki. Perhaps the alcohol would help to loosen his troubled thoughts and also provide some inspiration for him. It was early evening. The beach off to the left was still packed. There was a path leading off to the right that was much more appealing to him. Vasilis walked for a while and found a quiet spot to sit and look out at the sea, he took a long swig of the raki and his thoughts went straight to his wife in Australia. The last contact with her was three days ago, so much had gone down since then. Once again, he decided that it was better to leave things alone and not dig for information. He was certain that the police would have been in contact with her and as frantic as she would be, it would be best if he did not speak with her until things had come to a conclusion. A phone call could easily be traced, staying under the radar was his best option for now.

The raki had the desired effect, he was beginning to relax and feel more in control of things in general. It was a clear evening and he looked out to the neighbouring islands of Naxos and Paros on the southern horizon. For the first time in many years he was feeling his Greekness, he smiled as he thought of himself as a young man and the dreams that he once had. Life had taken many twists and turns for him and like everyone else he had skeletons in the wardrobe, but he was a survivor, and in his own mind he believed he was a good man.

He pulled the mobile phone from his pocket and replaced the sim card. After a few seconds the phone pinged to let him know that there was a voice message.

"Vasilis, it's Dimitris. Why have you turned your phone off? Listen, let me know when you get this. A girl was found at the apartment. What's going on? Call me!'

Vasilis sent a text message back to Dimitris. *"Got your message. I know nothing about the girl. I will be in touch. Trust me. Vasilis."* Then he removed the sim card again.

—⁓—

Naxos

It had been another long day of ferry travel for Mergim. Vlora had told him that they were coming close to the end now and that their prize was in sight. He was glad about that, but he also harboured a secret sadness. He had not accounted for his emotions. The more time that he spent around Katerina, the more he was falling for her. The other girls had made no impression on him, they were just victims, part of the big plan.

The whitewashed buildings of Naxos were visible in the distance and the ferry altered its course to line up with the harbour entrance. As he made his way down to the garage and the white panel van, he wondered what plans his sister had for Katerina.

He did not have to wait long for his answer. As he parked the van around the back of the villa, she stepped out of the rear door of the property and asked him. 'No problems?'

'No problems,' he replied.

Vlora looked back towards the villa. 'When it gets dark. Get rid of her.' Then she watched him closely for his reaction. Her prediction was confirmed, she continued, 'You are so obvious, big brother.'

Mergim fidgeted with the car keys and stared at the ground, trying to avoid eye contact with her.

Vlora leaned forward and tilted her head to stare into his eyes, 'Are you up to it? Are you capable of doing what I ask of you?'

He responded sheepishly, 'Yes Vlora, yes I am. I have killed once already, haven't I?'

'That was accidental. This one won't be.'

'How? I mean, what do you want me to do?'

'Your choice, Mergim. It was you that started this whole thing.' Vlora paused for a moment and added, 'If it helps, I can dope her up first.'

He nodded to show agreement with her offer, and as he stepped inside the villa, he asked her, 'When do we leave for Santorini?'

'We are taking the first available ferry tomorrow morning.'

Katerina had her ear pressed against the wooden panel of the locked door. She tiptoed away from it and back into the room. The only word she recognised was "Santorini."

The time had come for Mergim to take Katerina. Vlora unlocked the door and took their captive by her arm and led her to the kitchen. Mergim watched on as his sister presented a drink to Katerina and lifted it to her lips, 'Drink this, you must keep your strength up.'

Katerina drank the spiked fruit cocktail and placed the empty glass on the kitchen table. As she did so,

Mergim tied a blindfold around her eyes and moved her arms behind her so he could fasten her hands together with some gaffa tape. Katerina had dreaded this moment ever since she had witnessed the removal of Sophia. She wanted to scream and cry, but she stood tall and concentrated on keeping her breathing as shallow as she could. Vlora offered no words of farewell, she just held the door open for her brother as he guided the girl out to the panel van. Mergim opened the back doors and gently placed Katerina inside, then he climbed into the driver's side, stared back at his sister and nodded to her as he drove off.

Mergim stopped to buy some supplies at a supermarket in Kastraki, tins of sardines, fava beans and water. Once he was well clear of the village, he pulled over and shifted Katerina into the passenger seat at the front of the vehicle. He removed the blindfold and Gaffa tape from her hands. Her eyes were heavy, the effect of the sleeping pill was kicking in.

Mergim held her hand, 'Don't worry Katerina. I am not going to hurt you.'

She was fighting back against the tiredness, desperate to hear what he had to say.

'I am so sorry that you were dragged into this. You have to know that you were just unlucky.'

Katerina struggled to speak and simply uttered the name, 'Sophia.'

'Sophia is safe now.' Mergim squeezed her hand. 'I am going to take you somewhere, but it may be a few days before you are found. Okay?'

Katerina nodded and mustered up a half smile as a response.

Naxos had many small churches scattered on the highest points of hills all across the island. The church that Mergim selected was quite isolated. It was situated inland and only reachable by way of a single road that led up to the typical whitewashed building with its blue dome.

He arrived at the base of the steep hill that hosted the church and turned off the head and side lights for the van, the natural moonlight would be sufficient to navigate by. He waited for a few minutes to make sure that no one was around to witness his assent.

The door to the church was unlocked, not unusual for remote churches on the Island. Katerina was fast asleep by now and oblivious of her whereabouts. He moved her inside. He used the torch on his phone to light up the inside of the building. There was a strong musty odour combining with the smell of burnt incense. Two wooden pews situated along the side walls faced each other and a small alter lay at the end covered with icons and candles. Mergim knew that the church would only be attended by a priest on Sundays in order to light candles and say prayers. The nearest village was several kilometres away and unless there was a special occasion, like a name day, there would be no pilgrimages to the holy place by the villagers. It would not be comfortable for her, but she would be safe and, more importantly, out of the way until they had concluded their business on Santorini.

After setting her down on one of the pews and placing the supplies on the other, he knelt next to her and stroked her long dark hair as he thought of the last conversation that he had held with his mother. He used his lock picking skills to secure the church door before returning to the villa and his sister.

—~~—

It was a perfect evening for a ride on a motorbike. The air was still, the traffic was light and although darkness had set in, the visibility was good. Jordan did not feel the need for a helmet, besides he wanted to feel the warm night air on his face. He took the main coastal road past Kastraki and all the way south to Agiassos village, then followed it around as it tracked inland and back towards the north of the Island.

He was stopping at regular intervals to capture images, inspired by the landscape and the settlements that nestled into the hillsides.

The road opened up and he gunned the throttle. The speed and the thought of his forthcoming adventure with Maria in Santorini was stimulating his sense of freedom. He slowed down to navigate around a bend that swept off to the right. As he turned into the bend, a vehicle appeared out of nowhere. It came from his right side and cut across him. The vehicle had no lights on, so there was no indication of its approach. Jordan swerved heavily and just managed to bring the bike under control. He pulled off the road and watched as the offending vehicle accelerated away, as it did so its driver turned on the lights which lit up the rear. There was enough illumination to identify it as a van, but that was all.

Jordan cursed the driver and walked back to view the place where the van had pulled out on him. He located a road and followed its path upwards, a small church was situated at the top of the hill. He laughed to himself as he imagined that it could have been a priest that had taken just a shade too much raki. He was a little shaken by the incident, but he was okay and so was the bike, so no damage done. With that thought, he continued on his journey back to the Chora and dropped the bike and his belongings at his hotel, then he walked down to a beach bar that had become his favourite watering hole.

It was only 9.30 pm and the bar was still busy. Jordan glanced over to the barman, who in turn acknowledged his entrance and brought his usual ouzo and sprite order to the front of the drinks queue. Jordan took the last remaining seat at the bar and downed his drink in seconds. 'I needed that.'

'So I see,' said the barman. 'Another?'

'Yes please Yanis. I almost got knocked off the bike this evening.'

Yanis slipped another drink in front of him. 'Where? What happened?'

'I'd been out for a spin on the bike and was on the inland road, just south of Kastri. Someone pulled out on me on a blind bend. I think it may have been a priest in a van.'

Yanis laughed. 'A priest, what makes you say that?'

'I went back to have a look at the spot where it happened and the van had pulled out of a road that led up to a church.'

'Believe me, it wouldn't have been the priest. There is a religious festival in the town Platia tonight, all the priests on the island are in the Chora for the event. It's more likely that it was someone having an intimate moment, or someone up to no good.'

The image of the van accelerating away from the scene flashed into Jordan's mind. His stomach sank as he recalled that he had seen Mergim Vokshi driving a van earlier in the day. Then he discounted any linkage, surely he was letting his imagination get the better of him?

A drunken Danish tourist sitting next to him distracted him from his train of thought and opened up a line of conversation about Greek food. Jordan patiently chatted with the man over a couple more drinks, then he excused himself and left when he got fed up of pretending that he understood what the inebriated Scandinavian was talking about.

Vlora collected essentials and placed them into two backpacks and bagged everything else into three bin liners. She systematically worked her way through the villa, cleaning everywhere and removing any trace that they had been there. After making sure that the rear door was locked, she walked over to a gazebo, where she sat in the natural light of the evening. She heard the van approach and watched as her brother pulled onto the gravel parking area alongside her. Vlora went straight to the rear of the vehicle, opened the door and threw the loaded garbage bags into the back, then she climbed into the passenger seat alongside Mergim.

'Well. Where is she?'

He lied. 'I borrowed a rubber dingy from a quiet bay. She is about half a mile offshore, resting on the seabed.'

Vlora stared into his eyes and believed him. 'Good boy.' She punched him on his shoulder. 'I knew you could do it.'

He was keen to move off the subject and asked her, 'What's in the bags?'

'Everything that we don't need. We have to dump them and the van too. I'll follow you, find somewhere we can burn it out.' Vlora stepped out of the van and placed the two backpacks on the passenger seat. 'This is all we will be taking with us.'

The inland road was the best option, it was more isolated than the built up coastal area and had plenty of dirt tracks that wound their way up steep hillsides. Mergim was confident that his sister did not suspect anything. She followed behind on her motor scooter as they zig zagged up an incline, just south of the church where Katerina was safely imprisoned. Mergim stopped at an appropriate spot and turned the front wheels towards the edge of the road that sided onto a sheer drop. As he got out of the van, he cast his eyes in the direction of the church, everything looked to be intact. No vehicles or lights to be seen.

Vlora parked her scooter and removed the backpacks from the passenger side of the van. She instructed Mergim to pour petrol around the interior, torch the van, then push it over the edge so it would cascade away towards the road below. They both watched as it gravitated as a huge ball of flame and came to rest against a stone wall just short of the inland road.

'Perfect. Now let's get out of here,' said Vlora.

'Mergim jumped on the back of the scooter, pulled on his red cap and they headed off towards the Chora.'

Jordan's hotel was a few streets away from the beachside bar. He was feeling very mellow and pleasantly drunk as he weaved his way through the narrow lanes full of boutique hotels and restaurants. He turned to walk up a main road that led to a Platia and heard the familiar toot of a scooter horn warning him to step out of the way. As it flashed by him, he observed the couple on the machine, a girl driving and a male passenger wearing a red Olympiacos cap. He laughed and advised himself. 'I must start cutting back on the ouzo.'

✿

CHAPTER SIXTEEN

Thursday 13th June. Morning

Naxos

The Vokshi's had spent their last evening on Naxos in a cheap hotel room above a laundrette, a five minute walk from the port. Vlora awoke early and while her brother slept, she cropped her hair short and dyed it black. The blame shift onto Vasilis had gone a long way to move attention away from her, but she wanted to mini-mise detection by the police as much as she could. She knew she had taken a risk by allowing her picture to be taken by the girls on the ferries, but that was all part of gaining their confidence to open up about themselves. On reflection, it was not so much of a worry to her. After all, Katerina was dead, Sophia was silenced and Andrea had no link to her, other than a chat on a ferry.

Vlora looked at her image in the bathroom mirror, she liked the new look. It had been a frantic couple of weeks, but things were coming to a close. Within a couple of days it would be all over, and she and Mergim would be free to move on with their lives. Things could never be the same, but they could be proud of their actions.

She woke her brother at 7am, they had to make the 8am ferry to Paros where they would connect to Santorini.

~m~

Jordan's waking thought was that he had left the beachside bar without settling his bill last evening. There was no way that he wanted to get his barman friend Yanis into trouble, so he decided to return there to have breakfast. His second thought was how excited he was about going to Santorini. It would not be his first visit there, but this one was different, he was meeting with Maria, the girl that was occupying most of his daily thoughts.

The beachside bar was void of customers and Yanis was setting the tables and umbrellas as Jordan walked in.

Yanis looked up and smiled. 'I knew you'd be back.'

Jordan smiled back and responded. 'Add an omelette and coffee to my bill please Yanis.'

While he waited for his order to come, Jordan watched the early riser tourists taking a morning stroll or jog along the one kilometre stretch of beach. There was something special about mornings on Naxos and Jordan loved to witness the place as it slowly woke up. He would miss the tranquil mornings once he relocated to Santorini, for an island just a few nautical miles away, the differences were stark.

Yanis popped the omelette and coffee in front of him and asked. 'Have you recovered from your incident last night?'

'Do you mean the close shave on the bike, or the drunken Dane?'

Yanis laughed. 'The bike.'

'Gosh, it's the last thing on my mind today, Yanis. I am off to Santorini to meet a lovely lady.'

'Lucky you,' replied Yanis, then he asked him. 'Did you say that it was a van that pulled out on you?'

'Yes. A panel van. Why do you ask?'

'My cousin is a cop, apparently they found a burnt out white van close to where you said your incident was.'

Jordan laughed out loud and said. 'I think that priest needs some serious counselling.'

Jordan's satire was completely lost on Yanis. 'Sorry?'

'Don't mind me Yanis, it's just my weird sense of humour.' Jordan put on his serious face. 'Now that's a bit of a coincidence. Was anyone hurt?'

'Apparently not. Looks like it was set on fire and deliberately rolled down a steep hill. There is no way that any occupants could have got out.'

Jordan waited for Yanis to step away and quietly muttered to himself. 'Shit.' He hated the way his brain worked sometimes. His collective thoughts were drawing a picture for him, and it was of Mergim driving that van. There was only one way for him to discount any connection, and that was for him to go back to the scene and check things out. It was doable though, it was not far away and he still had the bike.

It was easy to find the spot where the van had pulled out on him, the church on the hill was the giveaway. Jordan dismounted and looked down at the tarmacked inland road. The tyre marks only covered a short distance, but they unquestionably belonged to his bike. He glanced up the hill towards the church, it was definitely where the van had come from, he had to investigate. The narrow road was steep and had a well-worn pathway alongside it, he guessed that the villagers had used that over the years in their pilgrimages to the holy place. He reached the church and killed the engine on his bike. The light reflection coming off the white-washed walls was blinding and seemed to generate a heat of its own as he stepped toward the blue wooden door, which was the only means of access or egress to the building. The church had no windows at all, just a narrow vertical opening that was reminiscent of an archer's window in a castle. The opening was situated under a large bell that hung from a frame on the roof.

Jordan tried to open the door but it was locked. He dropped to his knees to look through the keyhole. It was very dark inside, apart from a single shaft of light that was penetrating the interior of the church via the vertical opening. He got to his feet and placed his ear against a door panel and covered his other ear to cut out the ambient noise. There was no sound coming from the inside. Jordan banged on the door several times. If anyone was inside the church, surely they would have heard that. It was then that the more sinister thought came to him, perhaps there was someone inside but they were incapable of hearing anything at all. He dispelled the image of a corpse from his mind, but he knew he had to make sure there wasn't one in there.

The door of the church was designed to open outwards. It had an old mortice deadlock fitted, so it would take some force to break it open. He took a step back and looked at the church frontage. The rope for the bell ringer would do the job. He walked to the rear of the building and was able to scale the outer wall of the church at its lowest point. He untied the rope from the bell and threw it to the ground.

Jordan tied the end of the rope around the door handle and fastened the other end to his bike. Then he looked up and said. 'Sorry God, needs must. Oh, by the way, can you make sure that I don't just pull the door handle off?'

He edged the bike forward to take up the slack on the rope, then rode off to apply as much force as he could. It only took a short spurt of travel before he felt the resistance drop off. When he looked around to examine his work, the door had sprung open and he could see the shape of a young woman standing in the doorframe. His adrenaline was surging and it took him a few seconds to focus, it was Katerina, he had found her.

They said nothing, they just looked at each other, trying to come to terms with what had just happened. Then Katerina burst into tears and cried and cried. It was as if all the stress that had built up in her was coming out in one huge outpouring of relief. She had no idea who the person was that had just rescued her, until he put his arm around her and spoke. She looked into his face through her tears and hugged him, then repeated the same words over and over. 'Thank you.'

Jordan's reaction was very different. He could not contain his happiness and it came out as laughter as he comforted her. It was so ironic, he didn't even know if she remembered him from the restaurant and he had spent the last couple of weeks being obsessed with finding her.

Katerina reached up and touched the side of his face and said. 'I knew you would come for me.'

'Me? Why me?'

'I don't know. I just knew it would be you.'

Jordan looked over his shoulder and down to the inland road below. 'We can't stay here Katerina. We must get you away.' He looked back over to the church. 'Do you have anything in there?'

'Just some water and some tins of food.'

Jordan told her to bring everything with them. The door was hanging off the bottom hinge and he pushed it back into its frame to make its appearance look normal.

He reached over, took Katerina by the hand and smiled at her. 'Let's go.'

She held on to him tightly as he manoeuvred the bike down the steep access road for the church. When he reached the junction with the inland road, he stopped to think. Which way should he turn? Where was he going to take her? He was meant to be boarding a ferry to Santorini in a couple of hours, but this had changed everything. He needed time to think and talk with her. He made an executive decision and turned left towards the south of the Island. Jordan had regained his composure following the initial shock of pulling the church door off and discovering Katerina. He was thinking logically now. No cops, in fact, no phone calls to anyone, including Maria, not until he had ensured Katerina's safety. He recalled passing some studio apartments in Agiassos village when he was out on his ride last evening. They were situated off the road and the property edged onto a small beach. It would be an ideal place to hide out until he established the best way forward for them.

Thursday 13th June. Lunchtime

Vlora insisted that she and Mergim travel separately, on the same ferries, but not together. She had deliberately chosen smaller sized vessels, that way they could look out for each other, in the event that they were being followed. The tourist numbers were beginning to swell, as many Europeans made their move to the Greek Islands before the school holidays began. The Vokshi's blended in well with the visitors, it was hard to tell them apart with their backpacks and holiday style attire.

Jordan and Katerina reached the studio apartments. He drove the bike around to the front of the building and they dismounted. Katerina grabbed his forearm and stared at him.

He picked up on her fear. 'Don't worry. There is little chance they will be here. I need to get you inside and out of sight though. You better come with me.'

She followed him around to the reception area for the apartments but did not accompany him up to the desk, she waited by the door and kept an eye on the outside. Jordan asked if they had any vacancies.

The girl on reception looked over to Katerina and then back to him and asked. 'How long will you be staying?'

'One night will be fine.'

'It will be 75 for cash.'

'Thank you, that's great. Do you have a room on the first floor overlooking the sea?'

'That will be 90 for cash.'

He grinned and said. 'And it's available now?'

'Yes. Follow me, please.'

As soon as the receptionist left the room and the door closed behind her Katerina said, 'My mother. I want to call my mother.'

Jordan thought for a moment and replied. 'Sorry Katerina. That wouldn't be wise right now.'

She started to hyperventilate. Jordan was sure it was only a reaction to the trauma of her captivity. He sat her on the bed and told her to take deep breaths. He held her hand and said, 'Let's just take this one step at a time. We have to be very careful. Help me to understand what's been going on.'

She poured it all out, every detail that she could recall of her ordeal. When she reached the part where they had used the scalpel on her, she touched her neck and he slowly lifted her hand away to see what she was touching. The scar had healed but it was faintly visible, as was the pen mark that had been drawn on her throat.

Jordan recoiled as he made the connection with Andrea and Emilia.

Katerina witnessed his reaction and asked him. 'What is it?'

'Katerina, I don't think you know how lucky you've been. I am sure these people have killed a girl.'

It was Jordan's turn to explain everything that he and Maria had learnt. The information from the police courtesy of Mikalis, what they knew about Sophia, Andrea and Emelia, the villa in Halki and everything they knew about the Vokshi's.

'That's why we have to tell nobody yet.' He paused for a moment then asked her. 'How did you end up in that church?'

'He took me there. I am sure that she wanted him to kill me.'

'What makes you think that?'

'He bound and gagged me in front of her. Then he stopped the van and undid all of that. But it was the way he looked at me and the way he spoke to me. He was very nervous, like he was taking a risk by leaving me at the church. He said I would be found in a couple of days. That's all I picked up from him. I think they drugged me, I couldn't stay awake.'

'Do you have any idea where they are now?' said Jordan.

'They were very careful about what they said around me. But I overheard them yesterday, they were talking in Albanian, but they definitely mentioned Santorini.'

'Santorini? Are you sure?'

'Yes.'

Jordan reached forward and gently held Katerina by her shoulders. 'I have to call Maria.'

Katerina asked him. 'Can I talk to her, please?'

'Sure.' Jordan noticed that Katerina's eyes looked heavy, all of this was taking a toll on her. He told her to lay down on the bed and asked her. 'How did you know that I would be the one to find you?'

'I don't know. I think I willed it to happen. All I had for days on end was the darkness and my prayers.' Her words tapered off to a semi slur and she drifted off into a deep sleep.

CHAPTER SEVENTEEN

Naxos

While Katerina slept peacefully, Jordan gathered his thoughts, reflecting on everything she had told him. Why had she been spared? Should he go to the police and alert them that the Vokshi's were heading to Santorini? Had they even left Naxos? Then he recalled the couple on the scooter as he walked to his hotel last night. Could that have been the Vokshi's? He was back in the world of unknowns. The only person he truly trusted was Maria. Katerina was still in a deep sleep. Jordan stepped out onto the balcony and slid the door closed behind him.

He called Maria and jumped straight in when she answered. 'Maria, where are you? Can you talk?'

'I'm alone at my apartment, packing up my things. What's happening?

'I have some news. Katerina is safe, I have found her.'

'What! How, when?'

'Slow down. It's a long story Maria.' Jordan brought her up to speed with all of the happenings, including what Katerina had told him.

'I can't believe it Jordan, this is such good news.'

'How do we handle this though? By all accounts, she is supposed to be dead and we don't know where the Vokshi's are. Do we go to the police?'

Maria asked him. 'What does Katerina want to do?'

'I don't know, I haven't asked her.'

There was a knock on Maria's door. 'Hold on Jordan, someone is outside.'

Maria opened the door slightly. It was Mikalis. She held her finger up for him to give her a minute, then closed the door and walked across the room. 'It's Mikalis. What shall I do?'

'Find out what he wants Maria, but tell him nothing.'

'Okay. Will do. I'll call you back.'

Maria opened the door for Mikalis. He walked in and looked at her suitcase on the bed. 'So it's true Maria, you are leaving.'

'Who told you?'

'Come on, this is Koufonisia. Everybody knows what goes on here.'

She was not in the mood for small talk with him. 'So what do you want?'

'I couldn't let you leave without seeing you again.'

Maria just stared back at him without responding.

He took a seat at the table in her room and continued. 'Are you leaving to be with him, Jordan I mean?'

'What business is that of yours?'

'Well that's just it. I made it more of my business than I should of.'

Maria was getting impatient with him. 'What do you mean?'

'It wasn't my Sergeant that said he couldn't return here. I made that up, it was me.'

'Why on earth .....'

Mikalis cut her off. 'Because I was jealous of him. I have feelings for you Maria. I didn't want him around.'

'Okay, that explains a lot then.' Maria could see that he was being genuine. 'And I am sorry. But those feelings are only one sided Mikalis.'

'I realise that now.'

She walked over to him and hugged him. 'Thank you, for your honesty.'

He crossed the room to leave and looked back at her. 'Good luck and please let Jordan know that I have no hard feelings. I hope things work out for you.'

As tempted as she was to discuss the Katerina news, she held her tongue. Jordan had asked her to say nothing and this time she was not going to slip up.

Maria called Jordan. 'Hi, it's me. He's gone.'

'What did he want?'

'He came to say goodbye. He had heard I was leaving.'

Jordan asked nervously, 'You didn't say anything.....'

'No. You said not to.'

'Thanks. You and I need to talk with Katerina. We have to discuss the way forward with her. Her wants have to come first.'

'Agreed. Is she awake yet?'

'Yes.' Jordan went back inside and handed the phone to Katerina.

The girls talked at speed in Greek and lost him completely. He watched Katerina as she laughed and cried her way through the fifteen minute conversation. Then she turned to look at him and handed the phone back to him.

'Hey Maria, that looked emotional.'

Maria was sobbing and replied. 'Yes. Very. Put the phone on speaker so we can all talk.'

Jordan placed the phone on a table.

Maria led the conversation. 'Okay Jordan. Katerina does not want to go to the police. She is terrified of the girl, Vlora.'

Jordan reached out and touched Katerina on her shoulder.

Maria continued. 'Katerina told me that before they released Sophia, Vlora threatened her that they would get to her and her mother if she talked to anyone.'

Katerina cut in. 'I have to protect my mother. They know where she lives.'

'Okay. But how do we keep Katerina safe when we don't know where the Vokshi's are?' said Jordan.

'I am sure they are going to Santorini,' said Katerina.

Jordan said, 'Well it certainly looks like they have finished their business here on Naxos, disposing of everything before they leave. I'm almost sure that I saw them on a scooter driving through the Chora last night.' He asked Katerina. 'Does Mergim have a red cap?'

'Yes. He is never without it.'

'Look ladies. It's a bit of a gamble, but I think we should assume that they have business on Santorini and have gone there.'

Katerina said. 'Now that I know about the murdered girl on Amorgos, I am even more worried. Whatever this is all about, it is clearly not finished, otherwise they would have left the islands.'

'I agree,' said Jordan.

Katerina added. 'Plus, Mergim was prepared for me to be found in a couple of days, so whatever they are planning, it's happening soon.'

'So, if we don't involve the police, that only leaves us with one option. Jordan, you and I will go ahead with our plan to go to Santorini. We know what they look like, we should try and find them.' said Maria.

'And if we find them, what do we do?' asked Jordan. 'We have no authority, besides, Katerina is safe now, so why should we put ourselves at further risk?'

Katerina provided the answer. 'Because they have to pay for what they have done. We can't leave this open ended. How could I carry on with my life, knowing what I know and not doing anything about it? I can't go home and I'm not staying here all alone. I'm coming with you and we will find them and bring the police in when the time is right.'

Maria asked Katerina. 'And what about Vlora? What if she finds out that you are still alive?'

'I think we can work on changing my appearance and what's more, she won't be expecting to see a corpse walking around one of the busiest islands in the world.'

Katerina's comment brought some welcome laughter to the conversation. They agreed, they would all travel to Santorini and meet there on Friday.

꙳

CHAPTER EIGHTEEN

Thursday 13th June, Late Afternoon
Santorini

Vlora rolled off the ferry on her scooter and Mergim disembarked by foot. She rode up to the overpopulated bus loading area and waited for him to walk up and join her amongst the crowds of tourists. They took the only road out of the port and zig zagged up the steep incline that formed the backdrop to the busy port. They were enjoying the freedom of not having to transport human cargo. They also paid little attention to the wonderful vistas as they climbed to the top of the road and levelled out before heading to Kamari Beach, a busy resort on the east coast.

Vlora located a cheap hotel at the rear of the town, away from the beach front. She deliberately selected a family run place with rooms that were accessible off the street, without going through a reception area. She anticipated that they would be keeping strange hours over the next couple of days, and they needed the freedom to be able to move around without prying eyes on them.

Thursday 13th June, Evening

The time on Mykonos had given Vasilis the head space he needed. He had a simple plan. Get to Santorini before he was expected to arrive and, if his suspicions were correct, there was an obvious place that the antagonist would come looking for him. He would have plenty time to prepare himself for that confrontation.

It was 28 years ago when he last walked on this island. What struck him most was the sheer numbers of tourists arriving daily to Santorini. It was not even peak season yet and the ferry from Mykonos was packed solid.

Vasilis instructed the taxi driver to take him to the northern end of Imerovigli. There were several choices of family hotels there that would meet his needs. He chose one situated just off a main road that gave him ease of access to the major towns on the island. After settling into the room, he arranged with the owner to have a motorbike delivered to the hotel in the morning.

Vasilis picked the complimentary bottle of wine from the welcome pack in the room and took it out to the balcony. He had unspoiled views of the east coast of Santorini and the neighbouring island of Anafi. Vasilis removed the back panel from the phone and installed the sim card. Shortly afterwards, successive pings let him know that there were several messages waiting for him. They were all from Dimitris. *"Where are you?" "Are you okay?" "I'm concerned. Call me."*

Vasilis did not respond, he poured himself a large glass of wine, sat back, admired the views, and contemplated his plans for tomorrow.

—∿∿—

Friday 14th June, Morning

Naxos

Katerina had woken up several times during the night and gone into a panic, but that quickly subsided when she realised that she was safe and being guarded by her protector, Jordan. He had spent the night on the sofa bed, strategically placed between her bed and the door.

Jordan was impressed by her mental strength, it was hard to comprehend how well she was coping, considering the ordeal she had endured. He wondered if there would be a relapse at some stage. He suggested that they took a walk together to the nearby bakery to pick something up for breakfast.

Katerina only had the clothes she was wearing, the ones that were provided to her by Vlora. 'I need to get rid of these and put something else on.'

Jordan shuffled through his rucksack and pulled out a "I LOVE IOS" tee-shirt and a pair of his beach shorts. 'Try these on for size.'

She rolled her hair into a ponytail and, kitted in her touristy attire, they stepped out into the warm morning sun to make the short walk to the bakery. Complete with their purchases of coffee and Bougatsa, they sat on the deserted beach in front of their hotel.

The Island of Irakleia lay off in the distance, the place where Jordan had once met Maria for a picnic. As Jordan let his thoughts drift to Maria, his phone rang. It was her.

Maria said, 'Kalimera. What ferry are you taking to Santorini?'

'The big blue one that leaves at 1pm.'

'Good, I've decided to come up to Naxos this morning. I'll be joining you and Katerina. Buy me a ticket please.'

Jordan and Katerina were delighted. They could have their reunion earlier and they would also have another set of eyes available to keep Katerina safe, in the unlikely event that the Vokshi's were onboard the same ferry.

Jordan told Maria that he was going to return the motorbike and hire a car in its place. The car would provide better cover for them whilst on Santorini. In turn, Maria told Jordan that she would be bringing clothes for Katerina.

The reunion was emotional for all parties, but especially so for the girls. Jordan had missed Maria tremendously, but he was happy to wait and tell her that later. He made himself busy by loading Maria's baggage into the hire car and installing the dashcam to the windscreen.

As the newly reunited friends drove up to the ferry loading lanes, they scanned the queuing passengers and vehicles for any signs of the Vokshi's, but they were nowhere to be seen. It was a good sign, although Jordan did not know it, his assumption that they had left Naxos on Thursday was correct. The extra caution was worthwhile though, if only to help settle Katerina's nerves.

Afternoon

Santorini

The big blue ferry moored its stern against the concrete wharf at Athinios, the busy port for Santorini. Jordan waited for the signal from the crew member to proceed, and as he turned on the ignition, it simultaneously started the record function on the dashcam. It took all of Jordan's concentration to carefully steer through the oncoming traffic and passengers as he worked his way along the wharf. All of the Cycladic Islands were enjoying vast amounts of tourists now, but Santorini took it to a different level. The port areas of the islands had the same thing in common. They were full of trucks, taxis, buses, passengers and the hoteliers touting for business.

As Jordan manoeuvred past them and began the climb up the hillside, Katerina said. 'I think I have just seen them.'

Maria asked. 'Who?'

'The Vokshi's. I am sure it was them.'

'Where?' said Jordan.

'They were amongst the hoteliers, holding up a board with a hotel name on it.'

Jordan pulled over to the side of the road and stopped the car. He removed the dashcam from its holder and rewound it to the point where the hoteliers appeared on the recording. He paused it and handed it over to Katerina, who was seated with Maria on the back seat. She studied the image and placed her finger on the screen. 'It's them. There they are.'

Maria looked first, then Jordan. There was no doubt, it was the Vokshi's. But what were they doing posing as hoteliers? For whatever reason, that seemed less important than keeping them in their line of vision.

Jordan asked Maria to discretely go back and see if they were still there. She made phone contact with Jordan and provided commentary as she closed in on the diminishing line of hoteliers.

'They're still there Jordan. What do you want me to do?'

'Get back here Maria. But don't get into the car, try and keep them in your sight. We will try and follow them when they move off.'

Maria made it back to within a couple of metres of the car. She watched as a pair of tourists approached the Vokshi's. Vlora wasted no time in directing them away to the other remaining hoteliers. 'They're not interested in talking to the tourists Jordan.'

'Then they're here to look for someone specific Maria.'

Maria watched as the Vokshi's waited until the last few passengers from the ferry either boarded buses or taxis. The Vokshi's moved away and Maria informed Jordan.

'Okay Maria, good job. Get back in the car please. We'll follow them.'

—◊◊◊—

Vlora and Mergim mounted the scooter.

Mergim said. 'Do you think we missed him?'

'No. He wasn't on that ferry. He is probably here already. Don't worry, he will show up, he has no other option.'

Neither of the Vokshi's picked up that they were being tailed all the way back to their hotel in Kamari.

—◊◊◊—

Jordan tracked back to find the road up to Fira town, the capital of the Island. Maria had arranged an apartment there for them. He asked Katerina. 'How do you feel after seeing them again?'

She replied, 'Apprehensive, but pleased that we found them.'

Jordan directed his next question to Maria. 'What do you think? Is this the right time to involve the police?

'I don't know.' She thought for a moment and said. 'Do you think we can trust Mikalis?'

Friday 14th June, Evening

Santorini

So many years had passed since Vasilis had stood in the tiny secluded cove, but it looked exactly the same as it did then. As it was on that night, there was no wind and the only sound was the lap of the waves on the black volcanic sand. He stood facing out to the sea when he heard the words directed at him from behind.

'They say a criminal always returns to the scene of the crime.'

Vasilis held his stare out to sea and laughed out loud as he replied. 'Ah, Dimitris. You had me fooled for a while.'

'And you had me fooled for longer, Vasilis.'

Vasilis turned and faced the man that he had always called his oldest friend. 'Why Dimitris, why did you have to kill Emelia?'

Dimitris could not look him in the eyes, he turned his head to the side. 'That wasn't meant to happen.'

'Oh well. That's some consolation then.'

The two men stood in silence for a while as the tension built between them.

Vasilis broke the silence. 'So, we are here now. What's your plan?'

'It's you that should have paid for your crime, not Emelia.'

'Don't even utter her name, Malaka.' Vasilis took a step towards Dimitris. 'So are we even now? Don't you think this squares things up?'

'That's not up to me.' Dimitris looked him straight in the eyes. 'You have no idea of the misery and hurt that your actions have caused.'

Vasilis was considering rushing at Dimitris. But the words, "That's not up to me" prevented him from doing so. He had got it wrong, this was not just between him and Dimitris.

Dimitris asked him. 'So when did you realise that I was involved?'

'It wasn't until I broke away from your control that I realised that it was you doing the controlling.' Vasilis continued with a question. 'Why all the framing? The girl in the car, the girl in the apartment, why all of that? Why didn't you just confront me after the funeral?'

'You were given plenty opportunity to come clean. But no, you wanted to walk away again and head back to Australia. You had to be put in a position where you couldn't just walk away. You're a wanted man now. This time when you leave Santorini, you'll be paying for your crime.'

'So why don't you just turn me in now?'

'Like I said, your fate isn't just in my hands. Turn your phone back on and wait for my call tomorrow.' Dimitris turned to walk away, then looked over his shoulder and added. 'Have a good night's sleep and you may want to check the date tomorrow when you wake up.'

CHAPTER NINETEEN

Vlora City, Southern Albania

Donika had enjoyed a wonderful childhood. She was an only child and her parents adored her. Her mother essentially raised her on her own as Donika's father was a merchant seaman and spent long spells away from them. She was almost six when she realised why her father came and went so often. It did not affect their relationship though. They loved each other very much. He was a proud man and knew he had to do what he had to do to support his family. Her mother would always keep it a secret when her father was returning home from a voyage, but Donika would always know anyway. The night before he was to arrive, her mother would scrub the house from top to bottom and prepare his favourite meal, veal stew with cabbage rolls. As Donika reached the age of eight, she had learnt how to pretend nothing special was happening and to quietly go along with her mother's surprise.

The ritual was the same every time he returned. Her mother would come to the school and give an excuse as to why Donika had to leave early. Then they would go home together and her mother would open the front door and let her daughter go in alone. Donika would run into the arms of her father and they would hug each other for what seemed like forever. He would always have a present for her from some far off place in the world, which he would pull from his kit bag. She would sit on his knee and ask him where he had been and he would draw a picture for her and show her the many photographs he had taken on his voyage. She loved to see all the images, but one place was her favourite, Santorini. He had once sent her a postcard from there and she was fascinated with the place. She would always ask him, "Did you go to that special island Daddy?" On most occasions he would not have visited Santorini, but he always said that he did. He wanted to keep the magic alive for her.

She always told him that she would go there one day.

Donika was thirteen when her father died tragically in an accident at sea. It had been just another normal day for her until her mother and aunt turned up at school to bring her home and break the news to her. It was the worst day of her young life. Her father was her hero. He was her eyes for the magical places in the world outside of her village.

Life became difficult for Donika and her mother in the years following her father's death. Money was scarce and many sacrifices had to be made. They survived day to day and many neighbours and friends were kind to them, but the loss of the breadwinner was very hard. Losing the main male role model in her life at such an early age had a lasting effect on her, she was not sure about boys and tended to be shy around them.

As she was developing into a beautiful young woman, her mother hinted strongly that she should think about settling down with the right boy. It was the furthest thing from Donika's mind. She was set on seeing the world that her father had shown her and one place in particular was top of her list, Santorini.

She spoke two languages fluently, her native Albanian and as is common in the south of her country, Greek. She could also understand a little English, thanks to her father. Donika had her plan firmly fixed in her head, when she became eighteen, she was going to cross the border into Greece and head for Santorini and find work.

———

1991

Saturday 11th May

Vlora City, Southern Albania

Donika had worked hard to prepare herself for this day, both physically and mentally. It was going to be tough to leave her mother and the world that she knew. She knew in her heart that her mother did not want her to go, but she also knew that her mum loved her and would not stand in the way of her dream to go to Santorini. Donika was eighteen now and had left school two years earlier to take a job in a hotel. It was all about preparing herself for her adventure. Learning the ropes in the hospitality industry would set her in good stead for finding work in Greece.

Much had changed in her country in the last couple of years, many Albanians were seeking new opportunities in the wider world and Greece was a perfect choice for them. Entering Greece and finding legitimate work was a huge challenge, but there were ways and means. Donika's mother had family connections that could help her with those issues, including the supply of permits and visas. Although she did not want her beautiful daughter to leave, it was better that she gave her every advantage that she possibly could. Donika would not travel alone. Her mother made it conditional that a cousin would accompany her on the bus journeys, on both sides of the border. They would make sure that she had safe passage across the border and all the way to Athens. Donika was secretly pleased with this arrangement. This would be the first time that she had left Albania and she was scared. Plus, the company on the bus would be very welcome, as the travel time was more than 18 hours for the whole journey.

—•••—

Nothing could have prepared her for the farewell with her mother. She totally underestimated how emotional she would feel. This woman had been her rock, her wisdom, and she did not realise how much she loved her until this moment when she had to say goodbye. Donika repelled the thought that came into her head as she hugged her, of course she would see her again, this was an adventure and she would return to pick up where she had left off someday.

Donika's mood lifted considerably once she settled into her window seat on the bus. Her quest to see Santorini was about to begin, she had waited forever for this. Her cousin slept for most of the journey to the border with Greece, which suited her fine as she gazed out of the window to admire the mountains and countryside of her homeland. The border crossing was uneventful and passed without a hitch. She felt elated when she eventually crossed over into Greece.

The bus exchange occurred a few metres down the road from the border and she was met there by another cousin for the Greek leg of the journey. It got under way after an hour of waiting. The bus wound its way through cute villages and along mountain roads that offered panoramic views of the coastline and nearby islands, before it turned inland and through some bigger towns. Donika's cousin, Aleksander, had lived in Athens for a few months. He tried to show off with his knowledge of Greek life and Donika listened attentively to what he had to tell her, but she probably knew more about the place than he did. Donika had taken every opportunity to find out about Greece and its customs, in spite of living in a country that was extremely isolated from the world outside.

It was approaching midnight when the lights of Athens first came into view. The city was enormous and appeared to spread out as far as Donika's eyes could see. They seemed to be taking forever to drive through the streets of its suburbs, before they reached Syntagma Square and the bus terminal. Donika felt ecstatic when she stepped off the bus, it was 1am in the morning but the place was still full of activity. The fountain in the Platia and the Parliament Building were illuminated so beautifully and seemed to be welcoming her on a personal level.

Aleksander carried her case and they walked the short distance to Monastiraki and his modest apartment.

She would stay at his place overnight. The Athens night life was still in full swing and they made their way up to the Plaka district, where Donika caught her first site of the Acropolis. She was in awe of the city, its architecture and its vibrant feel. It had been a long journey and the emotions of the day had taken their toll, but she wanted to savour every moment. She mustered enough of a second wind to enjoy a late snack and a drink in a typical Greek taverna with her cousin, before calling it a night. She was living now, experiencing the world that her father had so loved.

Aleksander's apartment was on a busy corner above a restaurant and one block away from the main square in Monastiraki. The square was always a hive of activity and very popular with street vendors and people just hanging out together. Every street leading off the Platia was home to trendy shops, bars, restaurants and cafés. Donika had slept well, despite the street noise that went on until 3am. She woke from her slumber a little after 9 am, excited at the thought that this was the day that she would see her special island for the first time.

Aleksander escorted his young cousin to Piraeus, timing the 20 minute taxi journey so it arrived in ample time for Donika to purchase a ticket and board the ferry to Santorini. She hugged her cousin and thanked him for his kindness at looking after her. She was no longer nervous about being on her own, and as she stopped at the top of the boarding ramp to wave at Aleksander, she felt an excitement that she had never known before. The uniformed crew member instructed her to stack her suitcase in the section for Santorini, then directed her up the stairwell to the passenger decks.

The external seating area was very crowded but she did not care, she wanted to see as much as she could, so walking around the decks suited her. A siren sounded below and the ship's horn blew, the signal that they were about to depart. Donika rushed to get a standing place at the stern of the ship and managed to squeeze into a spot where she could lean on the handrail and watch the ferry sail away. She looked down at the water being churned up by the propeller and thought about her father, this was a sight that he must have seen so many times in his days at sea.

Athens had felt very stuffy and congested, and being on the open sea was wonderful in comparison. Donika watched as the mainland fell away and the first islands came into view. They passed many and stopped at a few on the way. The voyage lasted several hours, but at no time was she bored. The sea was calm, the weather was warm and there was so much to look forward to.

The ferry began its final leg of the voyage from Ios to Santorini, and Donika was desperate to catch her first sight of her special island. She moved to take up a viewing point on the port side of the highest passenger deck and waited patiently for the land mass to come into view. Her blood seemed to tingle in her veins as Santorini appeared on the horizon. At first she thought she was looking at snow perched on top of huge cliffs, but soon realised that they were whitewashed buildings and houses, like the ones that she had seen on the other Cyclades islands. As the ferry got closer, she could make out many of the blue domed churches that adorned the villages that crowned the now massive cliff faces. The day she had dreamed about so often had come, she had arrived at her paradise.

—ᴡᴡ—

Donika's cousin had given her some advice. "When you reach Santorini, the port will be very busy. Don't get caught up in the rush to get on the first bus for Fira. Go over to one of the cafés and let things settle down. People like to help others, try and get chatting with someone working there. Most of those folks will have been in your position before. Tell them that you are looking for work and somewhere to stay. It may take a couple of conversations, but someone will help you."

Donika smiled as she acted on Aleksander's guidance, he was so right. Everyone had piled off the ferry and targeted the three buses waiting a few metres away. It all looked very stressful as they jostled to squeeze onto the vehicles with their children and luggage. There were still a few hours of light left in the day as she took a table on the outside of a café. The view was incredible, a brilliant blue sky set above huge sheer rock faces that curved around for as far as she could see. The tempo in the port dropped off dramatically as the last of the buses pulled away. Donika looked up to see a young waitress standing by her side. The girl looked at Donika's suitcase and smiled at her. 'You are one of the smart ones then?'

Donika returned a confused look. 'Sorry?'

'I saw you wander over here. You are obviously avoiding the rush. It's a smart move, you would only end up in another scramble in the bus station in Fira if you got on one of those buses.' She continued. 'Are you here to work for the season?'

'I hope to.'

'Don't worry, you will find work. What type of work are you looking for?'

'Hospitality work.'

'That's a shame, we are really short of nuclear physicists here.'

Donika gave one of her confused looks again.

'Sorry, it's my warped sense of humour. What kind of hospitality work? Receptionist, cleaner, tour guide?'

Donika smiled. 'Receptionist or front desk would be great. I have experience.'

The waitress noted a likeable innocence in Donika, maybe because she saw an earlier version of herself in her. She excused herself and returned a few minutes later with a coffee and placed it in front of Donika. 'It's on the house.'

'Thank you. What time will the next bus for Fira arrive?'

'Half an hour or so.' The waitress paused for a moment and said. 'Look, it's up to you, but I finish in 20 minutes and my boyfriend is picking me up. We can give you a lift if you would like?'

Donika felt a pang of caution, but this girl seemed genuine. She replied. 'That would be so nice of you. Thank you.'

'You're welcome. By the way, I am Anna.'

Donika introduced herself and watched Anna as she went off to finish the rest of her shift.

—◆—

Vasilis was a handsome, strong built man in his early twenties. Anna chatted with him for a few minutes before bringing him over to meet Donika.

'This is the young lady I was talking about. She has just arrived and is looking for work. But first, she needs to find somewhere to stay tonight. I said we could take her up to Fira.'

Vasilis greeted Donika. 'Welcome to Santorini. We may be able to help you out with all of those things. What type of job are you looking for?'

Donika couldn't believe her luck, things were moving pretty fast. 'Hotel receptionist would be ideal, but I am willing to consider anything just to get started.'

Vasilis spoke directly to Anna. 'I think I may know a place in Imerovigli that's looking for someone. It's worth a try.'

Maria looked over at Donika and she returned an approving nod.

The road to Fira was full of hairpin bends, snaking its way to the top of the cliff that overlooked the port. The view got better and better at each turn in the road as the elevation increased. The first orange clouds were starting to appear high in the vivid blue sky, indicating that the sun was beginning its decent towards the western horizon.

Anna turned around to look at Donika. 'Is this your first sight of Santorini?'

Donika reached into her handbag and pulled out the postcard that her father had once sent to her. 'With my own eyes, yes. But I have had this card since I was a little girl.'

Anna took the card and looked at it. It was a beautiful picture, taken from the Santorini Caldera, on the cusp of sunset. 'That's wonderful Donika.'

Vasilis manoeuvred the car through the crowded main street that ran through Fira and continued up to

Imerovigli a few kilometres further north. They reached a strip of shops and restaurants and he pulled over alongside a hotel. He told the girls that he would be back in a few minutes, then he ventured inside.

Anna and Donika stepped out of the car and walked a few metres down the road that they had just driven up. Through a clearing in the buildings there was a view of the eastern side of the island. The terrain fell away sharply giving spectacular views all the way to the coast. Donika asked Anna. 'Why have we stopped here?'

'Vasilis's friend is the manager of that hotel. He's probably asking if they have any vacancies.'

'Really, that's so kind of him.'

Just as Donika made her reply, Vasilis came out of the hotel, accompanied by another man. They all gathered back at the car. Donika had led a sheltered life in regard to the opposite sex, but she had an instant attraction to this man. He was taller than Vasilis, with an athletic build, and he was much better looking.

Vasilis said, 'Donika this is my friend, Dimitris. He wants to talk to you about a vacancy at his hotel.'

It did not take Dimitris long to decide that Donika was the ideal candidate for the job on offer, besides, he too felt the initial attraction that only comes along once in a while. The good news for Donika was that the job on the front desk of the medium sized hotel also came with a room and board. She had been so fortunate.

Anna and Vasilis said their farewells and Dimitris showed Donika to her new abode. 'Meet me in the reception at 7am in the morning, take the evening off and relax.' He smiled and suggested. 'You may want to take a walk up to the Caldera and catch the end of the sunset.'

The Caldera was only a short distance away from the hotel. Donika stepped onto the street and orientated herself, she knew she would have to walk up the steep road ahead of her to get to the Caldera. She followed the road up past a church and a supermarket. The road forked at the supermarket and she carried on straight ahead, making her way through alleyways that snaked past expensive looking hotels and dwellings that she assumed belonged to locals. The terrain had levelled out and she took a right hand turn onto one of the best viewing places on the Island. The vista took her breath away. It was like she was looking down on the world. A red orange glow filled the sky as the sun dipped behind the island of Thirasia. The land mass, high cliffs with sheer drops, arched away to her left and right sides. Thousands of white buildings were nestled atop them. The glow from the sun lit up the white buildings, turning them into a range of colours, pink, blue, orange and red. Donika took the postcard from her bag and looked at the image. She realised that she was standing within a few metres of where that image had been captured. Did this mean her father was with her? She felt the warm tears rolling down her cheeks and watched as the sun disappeared and the light and colours gave way to a dark blue sky and sea.

✿

CHAPTER TWENTY

Saturday 15ᵗʰ June, 1991

Santorini

Donika was five weeks into her new life and loving it. She missed her mother desperately, but the regular letters helped to keep them bonded across the miles. Things had developed between her and Dimitris, but they had not gone public on their relationship. They felt it was best to keep it discreet in light of them working together and he being the boss. They were staggering shifts at the hotel, which gave them just enough time to miss each other and look forward to their next encounter. Time off was scarce and usually limited to late evening get togethers on the beach with friends, including Anna and Vasilis. Donika was so grateful for the kindness they had shown her.

Vasilis managed a bar on the east coast of Santorini, the lower side with the volcanic sand beaches. Donika liked him, he was Dimitris's best friend. He would often call into the reception of the hotel and ask for Dimitris. If his friend was not on duty, he would stay and chat with Donika. He amused her, he had a certain charm about him. But what she did not know and couldn't see, was that he was totally and utterly infatuated with her and had been from the moment Anna introduced her to him.

Donika had purchased a motor scooter and was making the most of her time off. She had settled into a nice routine where she would finish her shift and ride up to the village of Oia to watch the sunset, along with the hordes of tourists that would gather there every evening. Then she would escape the hustle and bustle and head down to the east coast to a small cove that she had discovered. It was a special place for her, serene and private. She would sit and look out to the sea and the nearby island of Anafi, reflecting on her new life and the man she was falling in love with, Dimitris. He would come and join her there and, after a while, they would go and find a taverna to have dinner, usually one without too many tourists though.

Evening

Donika parked her scooter by the roadside and made her way down to the beach by the narrow access pathway. She loved the sound of the black volcanic sand as it crunched under her feet. There was no wind. The sea glistened in the moonlight and Anafi presented itself gracefully on the horizon. She had only been sitting for a few minutes when she heard the sound of someone approaching from behind. It was a bit early for Dimitris, so she looked around cautiously. She recognised the frame of the man approaching her, it was Vasilis.

'Yasas Vasilis. What brings you here?'

He sat alongside her, bottle of ouzo in his hand. 'I like this place too.' He handed the bottle to her. 'Here, take a drink with me.'

'Oh, no thanks. I don't drink and I have the scooter with me.'

'Go on. One little sip is not going to hurt you.'

Donika felt both obliged and frightened and she reluctantly took a drink from the bottle. The sharpness of the alcohol stung her throat and she handed it back to him. She had not seen him like this before, he had been drinking heavily and was slurring his words.

He put his hand on her shoulder and said. 'So Donika, how are you enjoying Santorini?'

She was beginning to feel scared and gently lifted his hand from her shoulder.

He leaned forward to look her in the eye. 'Hey what's wrong, don't you like me? I thought you liked me?'

Donika tried to get to her feet and he pulled her down and said. 'Where are you going? I've only just got here.'

Her heart was pounding and she was finding it hard to speak but she replied. 'Look Vasilis, I think I need to go. I have to meet Dimitris.'

'Oh, him. Don't you worry about him.' He grabbed her by the hair and pulled her flat onto the black sand. 'I think it's time you showed me a bit of gratitude. You're having a good little life here now and that's thanks to me for getting you the job. Yes?'

Within seconds he was on top of her, pulling at her underwear and kissing her on her neck.

'Stop, please Vasilis. Please!'

He reached into his back pocket and pulled out a razor knife and placed it under her chin. 'Like I said, a little gratitude would be nice.'

She tried to shout but her word only came out as a whimper. 'No.'

He pressed the knife into her skin on the left hand side of her throat and dragged it down. The wound was not deep but it drew blood. 'Now. Take your clothes off.'

Donika did not move. She lay there terrified, unable to speak or react in any way.

Vasilis slapped her across the face and said. 'Then I'll have to do it then.'

He ripped at her clothing and as he raped her, he held the knife to her throat. He cursed at her, calling her a "bitch" and a "tease" and threatened to kill her if she told anyone about him and what he had done. When he finished, he stood and looked down at her. She was not moving, her eyes were wide open and they stared up at the night sky. He bent over to look at her throat and inspected the wound. The knife had penetrated her twice, the second one had left an incision across her windpipe. He used a piece of her clothing to wipe the stream of blood away and it revealed an L shaped laceration. It was too dark to make out how bad the cut was, but there was plenty of blood. He shook her by the shoulders and she did not respond. He looked around and they were totally alone. Vasilis dragged her the short distance to the rear of the beach and rolled her into some undergrowth, then he fled the scene.

—∞—

Donika lay unconscious for one hour before Dimitris arrived and discovered her. He carried her up the incline and gently laid her in the back of his car and drove straight to the hospital. The medics rushed her off to attend to her and he sat in the waiting area, trying desperately to understand what had happened to her.

After half an hour, a nurse entered the waiting area accompanied by two police officers. The nurse nodded towards him and the policemen approached him.

'Stand up,' came the command from one of them.

Dimitris got to his feet and looked over to the nurse and asked her. 'Is she okay? Please tell me she is okay.'

The nurse did not respond, she simply looked him up and down and walked off.

One of the policemen gripped Dimitris by his shoulders and the other placed hand cuffs on him.

'What's going on? What are you doing?'

They did not reply. They marched him out to the car park and placed him in their police van.

Dimitris' mind was racing and he felt sick as he realised that they thought that he had attacked Donika. Another half an hour passed and he was booked in at the Police Station and sitting in an interview room with a policeman and a Detective.

The Detective broke the uneasy silence. 'Go ahead then. Help us to understand why you did this, you animal.'

Dimitris responded. 'I have done nothing. She is my girlfriend. I found her like that on the beach.'

The Detective turned to the other policeman and sarcastically responded. 'Oh, of course. Why didn't we realise that?' He turned to face Dimitris. 'So that's okay then, we can all go home now. Now that you have told us that you're her boyfriend and that you miraculously found her raped and with her throat slashed?'

Dimitris was shocked. 'Raped?'

The Detective shook his head as if he was disgusted with the response from Dimitris, he turned to the other policemen and said. 'Lock him up for this evening, perhaps his memory will improve in the morning.'

———

Vasilis had gone straight to his apartment in Fira. He showered and bagged the clothing that he had been wearing and washed the blood off the knife. Then he changed into some fresh clothes and headed to the Caldera, ditching the blood stained clothing in a large bin as he passed the bus station. Then he crossed the busy road to get to the edge of the Caldera and hurried down the myriad of alleyways and stairways until he reached a church. The church was set in its own grounds and surrounded by a low white plastered wall. He made his way to the front of the church and leant over the wall. There was a sheer drop down to the sea below. Vasilis took the knife from his pocket and hurled it outwards into the night air and watched on as it fell away. It was far too high to see if it splashed when it hit the water, but it was gone.

As he climbed up the stairs and weaved his way back to the main thoroughfare that contained an array of restaurants and bars, he breathed a sigh of relief. He was due to meet with Anna in twenty minutes and decided to frequent a taverna that he used often, mainly to get himself noticed. Vasilis continued drinking and worked on the story that he would give to Anna as to why he had to return to Athens in the morning. The vision of Donika lying semi naked and bleeding on the beach kept flashing through his mind. He never intended to hurt her, but now he was thinking that it may be best if she was dead. On the other hand, if she lived, he felt that she would not talk, he had gone heavy with his threats and she looked terrified. Either way, he would not be hanging around to find out. If he was going to be implicated then he would have distance as an advantage. There were no overnight ferries, so he would have to endure the rest of the night and the early morning on Santorini. If the police did not come for him during the night, it would be a good sign.

Vasilis met Anna at the entrance to the Hotel Atlantis, just a few metres away from the taverna. 'You look lovely darling,' he said as he hugged and kissed her. Koukla, I have some bad news.'

'What is it, Vasilis?'

'It's my Grandfather. He is seriously ill, I have to return to Athens in the morning. They need me.'

Anna fell for it and agreed that he must go. 'Of course. Family comes first darling.'

'I don't know if I will get the chance to see Dimitris. If I don't, can you explain to him why I've had to leave so urgently.'

Donika had been lucky, the incisions were not deep and the sharp knife left a clean straight cut, so her wound had a good chance of healing in time, without heavy scarring.

When she came around, the nurse assured her that she was going to be okay. 'The police are here and they would like to talk to you, can I tell them to come in?'

Donika half smiled and nodded to give her approval.

The police told her that they were holding a man in custody. It was the man that had brought her to the hospital and that he claimed to be her boyfriend.

Donika was totally unaware of how she got to the hospital. But she told the police. 'My boyfriend is Dimitris. He had nothing to do with this.'

'Do you know who did this to you then?'

She shook her head and kept her silence. Donika was trying to black out her memories of the ordeal, but the threats made by Vasilis resonated loud and clear. She would never tell them. 'I have no idea. I was sitting on the beach and I heard footsteps behind me, that is all I recall. I think it was one person, but I can't say for sure.' She hated lying, but the alternative was worse.

The police asked her to give a description of Dimitris. They also gathered information about her personal details. Then they left and said they would be in touch.

Morning

Santorini

Vasilis was already on board the ferry and an hour away from the port of Santorini by the time Dimitris was taken back to the interview room.

The same Detective was hosting the interview. 'So. Where is your so called girlfriend from and how do you know her?'

'She's from Albania. She works at the same hotel as me.'

'And she is working legally in Greece?'

'Yes. We have her papers at the hotel. You can check with the owner.'

The Detective added. 'I am sure that you understand what an adverse effect that this kind of incident can have on our tourist business.'

Dimitris was smart enough to know where the conversation was heading and nodded to suggest that the Detective followed on.

'Your girlfriend has caused a bit of a problem for us, something we would rather not be dealing with. Of course, we can wrap it up easily if we have to. We have you as a suspect and it would be hard for you to prove that you didn't do this. But we would rather avoid all of that unpleasantness if we could.'

Dimitris followed his lead and asked the question he was meant to. 'And how do we do that?'

'The best thing all round would be if the problem simply goes away. You walk and she goes back to where she came from.'

'And what about the bastard that has done this? He just walks away too?'

The Detective responded with a shrug of the shoulders and a grin. 'Santorini is a very safe destination for the many thousands of tourists that come here, we all depend on that reputation. We can't let one isolated incident jeopardise that, can we?'

Dimitris was raging inside. The image of Donika lying in the hospital bed all alone was tormenting him. She had no one here. 'Are you saying that you are deporting her?'

'No. We have no reason to, but it would be better if she recovered somewhere else. There would be too many bad memories for her if she stayed here. Do you understand what I am saying?'

Dimitris could not believe what he was hearing, the tone of the Detective was threatening, he looked him straight in the eye and responded. 'Oh yes. I know exactly what you are saying.'

The Detective smiled. 'Good. Go to your girlfriend, give her the support she needs. And by the way, we have already contacted the owner of your hotel. He knows that she's been involved in an incident and that you are helping us with our enquiries. He isn't expecting either of you to return to work.'

☙

CHAPTER TWENTY ONE

Sunday 30th June, 1991

Aegina

Dimitris' sister Alexa had been so kind, she gave her brother and his girlfriend the run of her modest villa on Aegina. They had been with her for almost two weeks. She instinctively knew that something unpleasant had happened to the girl, but respected their desire to keep whatever it was to themselves. Alexa could see that her brother and his girlfriend cared deeply for each other and that made her happy.

Donika's scar was healing well. She wore a silk scarf around her neck to conceal the red L shaped wound that was a constant reminder of the horrific events of her last evening on Santorini. Dimitris was there for her in every way he possibly could be. But as much as she loved him, she knew that there was no chance for them. She was already preparing herself mentally to say goodbye to him, it was the right thing to do. How could they have a normal loving relationship after what had happened?

Dimitris had only asked her once about what had occurred on the beach that evening, and when she told him she had no idea and could recall nothing, he believed her.

It was 1am and he lay in bed, unable to sleep. The warm evening air was blowing in through the open window when he heard his bedroom door open. Donika had come to him in the night. She snuggled in next to him and whispered in his ear. 'I am so sorry my darling, but I have to go home.'

Dimitris knew the conversation was coming, but it did not make it any easier when it arrived.

Donika kissed him passionately and their warm tears ran down their cheeks and combined as they cried together for the first time.

Monday 1st July 1991, Morning

Alexa waived farewell to them from the pier as the ferry pulled away and set out on its one hour voyage to Piraeus. She had seen the sadness in her brother's eyes and wondered if he would open up to her about it one day.

It had taken less than two months for Donika's childhood dreams to be realised, then shattered. Now she was making the long return bus journey back to her homeland. Dimitris had been wonderful, giving up his job to take care of her and be by her side. She slipped her hand into his and smiled at him. They were approaching the border with Albania and only had a few minutes left as a couple.

Donika caressed his hand and said. 'I am going to be okay Dimitris, in a few hours I will be with my mother, she will look after me.'

The bus arrived at the border exchange point and Dimitris hugged her. 'Promise you will write to me Donika.' He paused for a moment and added. 'Who knows maybe one day......?

She put her finger to his lips to silence him and smiled. 'Who knows?'

Dimitris watched as she went through the checkpoint and headed towards the bus waiting on the Albanian side. As she stepped onboard, she waved to him. Then she was gone.

Dimitris boarded the bus to return to Athens. He settled into a window seat for the long journey. He had much to think about, not the least being how he was going to pick up with his life. Donika had made it clear that she wanted to return home to Albania alone. He was not inclined to return to the islands or to Athens either. Dimitris was drifting in and out of sleep when the bus driver announced that they were about to arrive in Ioannina. It was early evening, and as the bus navigated its way through the narrow streets of the outskirts of the city, the thought came to him that there were worse places to be. It was less than two hours to the border, and in time, Donika may agree to meet with him again. The thought brought a smile to his face. He reached up and grabbed his rucksack from the overhead rack, made his way to the front of the bus, and told the driver that he would be getting off at the stop in the city centre.

It took him no time to find a job, once again taking a management role in a hotel. After a few days he sent his first letter to Donika and patiently waited for something in return from her.

Thursday 1ˢᵗ August, 1991
Vlora City, Southern Albania

Donika's first month back in her home town was difficult. She never went anywhere without her neckscarf and it had become a part of her normal dress around the home also. The scar had faded markedly with the use of the special cream that she applied day and night.

Her mother was delighted to have her wonderful daughter home once again, but there was a tension between them that never existed before. Donika had become strangely aloof, saying very little about her experience on Santorini.

It all became too much for her mother when she discovered that Donika was locking her bedroom door on an evening. 'What is it Donika, what is troubling you?'

There was no point in holding out any longer, it would soon become evident, Donika confessed to her mother. 'I think I am pregnant.'

She waited for her mother to explode, but it never came. A calm response filled the void after a few seconds. 'Who and when? How long gone are you?'

Donika was desperate to avoid the truth and lied. 'It was someone I met in Santorini, a tourist. I didn't go looking for it, it just happened, it felt right. I have only missed one period. I never miss them.'

'I will deal with this Donika and you will do as I say. You will not bring disgrace onto our family.'

—⁓—

The return address for Dimitris puzzled her at first but Donika soon worked it out that his relocation to

Ioannina was based on a hope that they would reconcile. He wrote every week and she had not replied as yet. The truth was she did not know what to say. He was the love of her life, but did not deserve to be involved in her mess. She had to be cruel to be kind. When she eventually replied, she told him that they could never be more than friends and that he must find a way to move on with his life. Dimitris never wrote to her again, although Donika still secretly hoped he would.

Saturday 3rd August 1991, Afternoon

Donika returned home from shopping to discover they had a guest. Her mother was entertaining a man in the living room. Her mother called her. 'Please join us, Donika.'

Burim Vokshi was ten years older than Donika, ruggedly handsome, but not really her type. He stood to greet Donika with a smile and a polite nod as she stepped into the room and waited by the doorway.

'Please come in, take a seat with us,' said her mother.

Donika smiled at them both and took a seat closest to her mother.

'This is Burim Vokshi, his family and ours have been friends for many years.'

Donika had absolutely no idea who he was, but listened respectfully as her mother continued.

'He and I have spoken at length about you. We think it would be a good idea for you to get to know each other.' With that, her mother left the room and closed the door behind her.

Donika could only raise an awkward smile at the stranger. She found it almost impossible to say anything as there was so much going on in her head. After a few seconds she stood and said. 'Would you excuse me please?'

Burim said nothing in return, but acknowledged her request with a nod.

Donika located her mother in the kitchen and closed the door behind her. 'Am I thinking what you are thinking mother?'

'He is a good man, Donika. He knows about your condition and is prepared to support you, and this family. What other choice have you left us with?'

Donika ran out of the house, her heart was thumping and she wanted to scream. 'What had become of her life?' she thought as she wandered through the neighbourhood that she knew so well. She crossed over a busy road and reached the edge of the cliffs that overlooked the busy coast road and the huge bay that connected to the Adriatic Sea. Donika leaned forward to look at the traffic on the road below, her thoughts frightened her and she stepped back. She placed her hand on her belly and thought of the new life growing inside. Looking out to sea, she saw a ship sailing past the headland opposite and thought of her father. Then she turned around and walked back home.

When she re-entered the house, Burim had left. Her mother opened her arms and Donika went over to accept her embrace and she let her tears flow.

'That's it. Let it all out,' her mother said. 'Give it a couple of days my angel.'

A couple of days made a big difference. Donika had offloaded one of her worries and her mother was doing her best to help her. She was beginning to think in a more pragmatic way. There was no way that she could support herself, a child and her mother. If Burim knew about her pregnancy and was prepared to accept it and take her on, then perhaps it was worth considering. She asked her mother to contact him and arrange another meeting.

Wednesday 14th August 1991

Donika had met with Burim on several occasions and his kind ways had grown on her, she was slowly allowing herself to admire him. Her mother was keeping a close eye on developments and never missed an opportunity to promote his qualities to her daughter.

'Donika, you must not allow things to progress too much. It won't be long before you are beginning to show. Burim may not wait around too long.'

'I have already made my mind up mother. We need to find a wedding dress.'

March 17th, 1992
Vlora City, Southern Albania

Burim and Donika were excitedly awaiting the birth of the child. They were living with Donika's mother and life was good. Burim was a hard worker and he had fallen deeply in love with his young bride. He had long since come to terms with the fact that the child was not his. How could he not forgive her for a careless liaison during a holiday romance? As he witnessed the new life growing inside of his love, he felt a sense of responsibility and was looking forward to being the best father that he could be.

Donika had learnt to mask her emotions and keep the lie buried. On the bad days, she would blame the hormones for her mood swings. On the good days, she rejoiced at the thought of bringing her child into the world. A grandchild for her mother, and a little human that was a part of her father too.

It was Donika that chose the name for the new arrival, he would be called Mergim. A common name in Albania that means stranger or foreigner.

Burim was a good stepfather to the boy, but always longed to share a child of his own with Donika. In April 1997, his wish came true, when they celebrated the birth of their beautiful girl, Vlora.

As the years went by, Mergim and Vlora became very close and family life in the Vokshi household was generally good. Then it changed. Burim began to show aggressive tendencies towards ten year old Mergim. Blaming him for anything and everything, even if the boy was not at fault. Vlora received no such attention, she could do no wrong in her fathers' eyes. A tension was building between Donika and Burim and it reached its climax one year later.

Burim had just finished reading a bedtime story to six year old Vlora. When he returned to the living room, Donika was waiting to talk with him.

'Why do you treat our son the way you do?'

Burim held his tongue, he was in no mood to get into an argument. But Donika wanted to clear the air. He turned the volume up on the television and avoided eye contact with her. Now was not the time for him to discuss this with her.

She turned the television off and stood in front of him. 'I am talking to you Burim. Why do you give Mergim such a hard time?'

'Have I been a good father to him? Have I provided for him?' his tone was becoming aggressive.

Donika responded with a smile and tried to defuse the tension. 'Of course you have. What is really wrong here, Burim?'

He walked out of the room and returned with several letters in his hand. Donika's heart sank as she watched him throw them onto a table. They were the letters that Dimitris had sent to her from Ioannina. Although there was no direct mention of the rape, there was enough information in them to reveal that she had not told the truth about the conception of Mergim. Burim had found them a year ago, tucked away in the bottom of her old suitcase. Rather than confront her there and then, he allowed his imagination to run wild, concluding that she had abused his kindness and taken him for a fool. He festered on it and as the months went by, it eventually formed into a deep routed hatred for the woman he had given his heart and life to.

It was another bad decision in her life, she should have destroyed the letters. All she could do was stare back at him and wait for what he was about to say next.

'So, what does this Greek friend of yours mean when he talks about your ordeal and your recovery?'

Donika had little option other than to come clean with him. In all the time that she was with Burim he was never allowed to touch her neck, she told him that it was extra sensitive and she did not like the sensation. She removed the silk scarf that was ever present on her neck during daylight hours. Their lovemaking was always conducted in the dark, so he was seeing the remnants of the scar for the first time. It was faint, but still visible.

'And what is this?' he said.

She blurted the truth out. 'The man that raped me did this.'

There was silence as Burim allowed her confession to sink in. Then he erupted. He ranted at her, telling her that he could not understand why she had not been truthful with him from the start. He screamed at her that she had carried the child of a rapist and allowed him to think that it was conceived out of some kind of loving affair. He accused her of allowing him to raise the child of another man, an evil man. A child that was probably cursed.

Donika had no response, she just wept through his barrage of abuse.

As Burim turned to exit the room he directed his vengeance onto Mergim. 'And that boy, I treated him as my own son. I tell you now, after what you have told me. That boy is evil. You will see, he is evil.'

Donika followed her husband into the bedroom and as he packed his belongings into a suitcase, she begged him not to leave. Her pleadings had no affect and Burim deserted the family that evening.

In the months that followed, Donika expected Burim to return. Surely, he would come back to see his daughter? The months turned into years and Burim never showed up again.

🜨

CHAPTER TWENTY TWO

2018

Mid December

Vlora City, Southern Albania

Mergim sat at the side of the hospital bed, watching his mother as she battled with the cancer that was going to cut her life short. Donika was only in her mid forties. He had travelled back to Albania from Greece after receiving a message that she wanted to see him. He reached out and touched her hand, which had the effect of rousing her from the light sleep she was in.

She manoeuvred her hand to grip his and said. 'Thank you for coming, son.'

Mergim responded with a smile. He had moved to Greece for work six years ago and rarely travelled back to his homeland. For as long as he could recall, they never shared a close loving relationship. Mergim was close to his Grandmother, but she had passed away when he was eight. The relationship he treasured the most was the one he held with his sister, Vlora. She was also working in Greece, studying medicine. He was very proud of her. Vlora had not accompanied him back to Albania, his mother only wanted to see him.

Donika knew that the disease would take her soon and that it was time to talk to her son, there were things he had to understand. 'My son, I know I haven't been a good mother to you. I need you to know that none of that is your fault.'

He had never understood her mood swings or the way she treated him, but he just accepted it, it was how it was. 'Mother. You don't have to …….'

'No son, please hear me out. I made decisions in my life. I chased my dreams. For whatever reason, my dreams did not work out.'

Mergim knew from conversations with his Grandmother that his mother had gone off to Greece as a young girl and returned to Albania and was married shortly afterwards. He said. 'Things don't always work out the way we want them to.'

'I paid a huge price for following my dreams son, and so have you.'

'What do you mean?'

'I have never been able to show you the love I wanted to.'

'Why?'

Donika explained how he had been conceived and how she had kept the secret covered up. A decision that had massive consequences, that resulted in her husband deserting them. 'I am so sorry that I have to tell you this Mergim, but I cannot die with this guilt on my conscience.'

Mergim was devastated by the news, but his overwhelming emotion was that of the sadness he felt for his mother. Donika reached up and wiped the tears from his cheeks and he stood up to cradle her in his arms.

She asked him. 'Please open the drawer in the cabinet. There are some letters in there.'

He removed the letters from the bedside cabinet and handed them to her.

'The man that wrote these letters is called Dimitris. He is the only man I have ever loved. I wanted to be with him, but I pushed him away Mergim. I would like you to find him if you could.' She turned one of the letters over to show some writing on the back of the envelope. 'He has a sister, she lived on the Island of Aegina. This is her address. He could be anywhere, but I feel she will still be on Aegina. Promise me you will try and find him and bring him to me.'

'I will find him mother, I promise,' said Mergim.

'One more thing, son. Don't tell your sister about any of this. She doesn't have to know. Okay?'

'Yes.'

Dimitris' sister Alexa was still living at the same property on Aegina. She was delighted to meet the son of Donika and very happy to give him the contact details for her brother. He was living and working in Piraeus. Mergim waisted no time in going to meet with him.

Dimitris could not believe that he was looking at the grown up son of Donika. 'This is amazing. After all these years, what brings you to see me? How is your mother?'

The news of Donika's condition upset Dimitris greatly. He had never married. He remained in Ioannina for a few years after receiving the rejection letter from Donika. There had been other women in his life, but none that compared to her.

'Will you come to Albania with me?'

There was no question about it in Dimitris's mind. He had to go and see her.

———

Early January, 2019
Vlora City, Southern Albania

Mergim entered the hospital room alone. His mother was sitting up in bed. She looked so pleased to see him. 'I have brought you a visitor.'

She smiled broadly when she asked him. 'Is it Dimitris?'

'Yes. I think it's best if you talk alone. I will send him in.'

It was more than twenty seven years since Dimitris had waved farewell to Donika at the border, and the years had not diminished the love that they held for each other. The years had been good to Dimitris, he was still the handsome man that Donika remembered. Her face lit up as he entered the room and rushed over to her. They talked, laughed and cried together for the best part of one hour, before Donika broached the uncomfortable subject.

'Please forgive me for what I am about to tell you Dimitris.'

He looked confused but nodded to indicate that he would.

'That night on the beach in Santorini. I have always known the identity of the person that raped and assaulted me.'

Dimitris was shaking his head now as if to doubt what she was telling him.

'Up until now I have never told a living soul who it was. But I'm not taking it to the grave with me.'

Dimitris gripped her hand with his.

'It was Vasilis.'

'Vasilis? Vasilis Kostas?' Dimitris was visibly shocked. 'Why Donika, why did you not tell me?'

'Oh, I wanted to, believe me. But I couldn't.'

'Why? I don't understand.'

'He threatened to kill me and almost did.' She touched the faint scar on her throat. Plus, if I had told you, I was afraid that you would kill him and ruin your life.'

Dimitris felt a rage inside that he had never experienced before. He exhaled a deep breath, the rage could wait. Right now he was with the woman he loved and they had to make the most of the few precious moments that they had left together.

—•—

It was only three weeks later when Dimitris returned to Albania for the second time in his life. On this occasion it was for Donika's funeral. It was only a small affair, a few cousins, ex neighbours, and Mergim and Vlora.

Dimitris met Vlora for the first time, she resembled her mother but there was a hard edge to her, something about her that she did not inherit from her mother. There were things he wanted to say to them, but decided to run them by Mergim in the first instance as he had already established a relationship with him, the conversation would be easier. Dimitris arranged to meet with Mergim in Athens, they could talk freely there in a weeks' time, once things had settled down.

—•—

Mergim listened carefully to what Dimitris had to tell him, revealing the details about the happenings on Santorini in the summer of 1991. He explained how he and Vasilis had become estranged for a few years after that, and picked up with their relationship once they were both living back in Athens. Dimitris talked about his plan to force Vasilis back to Greece from Australia and bring him to justice. Mergim was totally sold on the plan and he agreed to run it past Vlora. If she was okay with it, then they could all meet and thrash out the details of how to execute the plan.

Dimitris had remained friendly with Vasilis's ex-wife and he was well aware that Emilia was intending to take up a summer job on the islands. His plan would be plotted around that piece of knowledge.

When they all met two weeks later, Vlora became the driving force to model the fine detail of what, how, where and when. With the exception of Emilia, the others would be selected based on chance and opportunity.

༅

Chapter Twenty Three

Saturday 15th June, 2019. Morning
Santorini

Jordan, Maria and Katerina reached a compromise. It was too early to involve the police directly, but there was too much at stake to try and manage the situation on their own. They all agreed that it was worth the risk to call Mikalis, and they did so from their hotel room in Fira yesterday evening. He had listened without comment until they gave him a full brief on the situation. When he reacted, he told them that they had done the right thing all the way along the line, but they could no longer take this on by themselves. He suggested that he would join them in Santorini, it was his weekend off and he would not be missed on Koufonisia. He had a plan and would share it with them once he got there.

―⁓―

Midday

Mikalis rendezvoused with them at their apartment in Fira. The first person he approached was Jordan.

'Thank you for giving me another chance.' As they shook hands Mikalis said. 'Can we put the past behind us?'

Jordan smiled. 'It's gone, Mikalis.'

Mikalis turned to Katerina. 'I am sorry we let you down, Katerina.'

Katerina responded. 'Let's make sure they don't hurt anyone else.'

Mikalis smiled at Maria and said. 'And thank you Maria, for trusting me.'

Introductions over, they all sat around a table and listened as Mikalis addressed them. 'I think your conclusions are correct. With all the girls accounted for, there is no need for them to still be in the Cyclades, unless they have unfinished business. Plus, it really appears that they were looking for someone at the port yesterday.'

'Do you, or the police, have any indication of who that may be?' asked Jordan.

'Based on what you have told me, I would be willing to bet that it is Emelia's father. He is already linked to the case through Sophia and Andrea. But with everything Katerina has told me, there appears to be some sort of connection to the Vokshi's. But what is not obvious is how or why.'

Maria asked Mikalis. 'So, what do we do now? Do we alert the police on Santorini?'

'Yes, if we only want to capture the Vokshi's. But no, if we want them to lead us to whoever else is involved in all of this.'

'Then with all due respect, I think that call is yours Mikalis,' said Jordan.

Mikalis acknowledged Jordan's remark with a smile. 'Then here's the plan. Maria and I will go to Kamari and perform some boring police surveillance work on the Vokshi's. Jordan, please stand by here with Katerina. If we need you, we will call you.'

―ᰔᰔ―

Kamari, 3pm

It had been a long three hours, but the Vokshi's eventually emerged from their room. Wherever they were going, they were going on foot. Mikalis gave them a head start and he and Maria got out of the car and followed them down the narrow lane that led towards the beach front of Kamari. Small boutique hotels, tavernas and trees lined the lane, all playing a part to provide shade from the intense afternoon sun. Mikalis gripped Maria by the arm as he noticed that the Vokshi's had slowed down and stopped to speak with a man. The trio embraced in Greek style with a hug and kiss on both cheeks before entering a taverna.

'Looks like a lunch meeting,' said Mikalis. 'Let's join them.'

Maria's jaw dropped and Mikalis laughed. 'Don't worry, they don't know us. We will sit a few tables away from them.'

Maria said. 'She may remember me from the ticket office in Koufonisia.'

'Then keep your cap and sunglasses on. You can also sit with your back to them.'

Maria's nerves soon settled once she and Mikalis took to the table on the opposite side of the taverna. Vlora had her back to them and Mikalis had a front on view of the man that was with him, allowing him to take several discrete shots with his phone camera.

Mikalis zoomed in on the image and declared to Maria. 'That is not Emilia's father.'

'Are you sure?'

Mikalis flicked through images on his phone and placed the phone in front of Maria. It was a copy of the passport photo of Vasilis Kostas. 'He is on our wanted list, remember?'

The man was doing most of the talking and the Vokshi's listened on for the best part of twenty minutes before they all stood to part company.

Mikalis informed Maria. 'They're leaving. Sit still for now.'

The trio headed to the exit and chatted for a couple of minutes before the Vokshi's turned back towards their hotel and the other man went in the opposite direction.

'Shit,' said Mikalis.

'What's wrong?' asked Maria.

'The Vokshi's are between us and the car. Malaka.' Mikalis stood up and told Maria. 'Wait here.'

He moved swiftly onto the street and followed the man down the lane. The man got into a car and Mikalis took a photo of it and sent it to Jordan. Then he called Jordan. 'This is going to be a long shot, but I've just sent you a picture of a car. Make your way down to the junction where the Fira road meets the road coming out of Karterados and look for that vehicle. If he is heading back to the Caldera then he will most likely take that road and should be there in about 10 minutes.'

'I'll do my best. If I see him, what do you want me to do?'

'Follow him, if he stops, stay close and don't lose him.'

'Do I take Katerina or leave her here?'

'Take her, you will need her to give you directions. Make sure she is disguised though. Got it?'

Jordan replied, 'Got it.'

Mikalis ended the call and ran back to the taverna. Maria was waiting for him by the entrance. 'I've paid the bill and I watched the Vokshi's, they have gone back to their room.'

He laughed. 'Good work detective. Now let's get to the car.'

Mikalis could not help feeling proud of himself. He'd gone from mundane police duties on Koufonisia, to being in charge of a fast moving investigation on Santorini. He knew there would be a price to pay for not disclosing information and going out on his own, but that was for later, he was in too deep now. Mikalis explained what he had instructed Jordan and Katerina to do and told Maria that they would continue with the surveillance role on the Vokshi's. As Maria and Mikalis settled back into the car, the phone call came in from Jordan.

'We are here and watching.'

Mikalis checked the time display on his phone. 'You made good time. If he is coming, he should be there soon.'

A few seconds later Jordan said. 'And here he is.'

'Get on his tail Jordan. We are staying here. Be careful not to get spotted.'

'Talk soon,' said Jordan.

Dimitris turned right and joined the road that would take him to Imerovigli and his meeting with Vasilis. He had called him to arrange it after conducting his meeting with the Vokshi's.

There was not a lot of traffic on the road and Jordan kept a safe distance behind him. Jordan's phone pinged and Katerina responded to it. Mikalis had sent an image of the man in the taverna with the Vokshi's, with the message. *"Do either of you know this person?"*

Katerina replied. *"No. We've never seen him before."*

When Dimitris reached Imerovigli, he slowed down and stopped opposite a hotel. He didn't get out of the car but appeared to take a good look at the place for a few minutes. Jordan waited patiently behind him. Dimitris moved off and drove a short distance to a crossroads where he parked the car and got out.

Jordan used his camera to take some close up shots of Dimitris, then he called Mikalis. 'Our man is heading up towards the Caldera at Imerovigli, we are going to follow him on foot.'

'Good. Just act like tourists. There's no movement here, we are going to wait it out unless you need us up there. Okay?'

'Sure. We will let you know.'

The church, the supermarket, the hotel and the streets looked just the same as they did when Dimitris set eyes on Donika at this place, all those years ago. Now she was gone, ahead of her time. He wondered if the stress of everything she had endured had anything to do with her failing health and the cancer that took her. Irrespective of that, Vasilis had much to answer for and that time was coming very soon. He reached the end of the pathway and entered the upmarket hotel with unspoiled Caldera views.

Jordan took Katerina by her hand and picked up the pace to keep up with him. They stopped level with the entrance to witness their man being directed to a table at the front of the restaurant section of the hotel. The entrance was a gap with stairs in between a continuous high wall, they would be too conspicuous if they remained there.

Jordan said. 'We have to find a vantage point to give us a view over that wall.' Katerina looked around and discovered a bell tower for a church situated right behind them. 'Will that do?'

'If it's open, that will be perfect.' Their luck was in, the door at the base of the tower was not locked. Jordan directed Katerina to enter first and make sure they had access to the top before he took his eyes off the hotel. All was good and they proceeded to the top. They smiled at each other as they took in the magnificent views before turning their attention back to their man. Jordan checked him out, using the zoom on his camera. The man was alone but sat at a table that was set for four. It was Katerina that spotted another man entering the hotel and alerted Jordan, who in turn started clicking away with his camera. They both watched as the second man approached their man and took a seat opposite him. There was no traditional greeting, just a prolonged look at each other. Jordan zoomed in with his phone camera and managed to capture a side view of the second man. Then he sent it to Mikalis.

Jordan's phone rang, it was Mikalis. 'That is Vasilis Kostas. What's happening there? Where are you exactly?'

Jordan replied. 'We are up a bell tower, overlooking a swanky hotel. We followed our man there and now this Vasilis Kostas has just joined him. They're seated in the restaurant area.'

'Good work,' replied Mikalis. He paused for a moment and continued. 'We have movement at our end. The Vokshi's are on the move.'

'What's the betting that they are coming to join our men here. The table is set for four,' said Jordan.

'Could very well be,' said Mikalis. 'They're getting on the scooter now. We are going to tail them. Stay where you are.'

Dimitris deliberately held the uneasy silence, he wanted to force Vasilis to speak first.

'So, 28 years apart and we get the same day, month and date.' Vasilis was smirking as he followed on. 'So why did you wait so long?'

'Save your questions for when our company arrives.'

Vasilis laughed. 'Oh, so you think I am just going to confess to the police? Put my hands up and incriminate myself, just like that?'

'Why do you think it's the police that's coming?'

'Isn't that it? You've brought me here to the scene of the crime, as you call it. This is your idea of justice.'

Dimitris responded coldly. 'Your words, not mine. Now shut the fuck up and wait until our company arrives.'

The motor scooter was able to park closer to the hotel, using the side of the pathway as a parking place. Jordan and Katerina watched from above as they dismounted and went into the hotel. Mikalis and Maria were following behind, having parked their car beside Jordan's at the crossroads.

Mikalis glanced up at the bell tower and called Jordan. 'Looks like you were right. Here they all are. No point in us coming up there. Keep the line open and let us know what's happening.'

———

Vlora and Mergim arrived at the table and Dimitris stood up to greet them. Vasilis remained seated. As the Vokshi's took to their seats Vasilis smirked once again and asked, 'So if you are not the police, who the fuck are you?'

Dimitris calmly contained his anger and smirked back at him. 'Vasilis, let me introduce your daughter's killers.'

Vasilis went straight into a state of internal rage but held his temper and did not reply. He simply stared at Vlora and Mergim, who both returned a cold expressionless stare.

Dimitris filled the silence. 'These fine people are the children of Donika.'

The trio all watched the dramatic change of expression on Vasilis's face. He was clearly shocked by the revelation that Donika had not died on the beach that night.

'Yes Vasilis, you left her for dead. But she survived,' said Dimitris. 'Is there anything you would like to say to her children?'

Vasilis stared out at the vibrant blue sky and sea. 'You are all jumping to conclusions. You have no idea what happened that night. She was cheating on you Dimitris, she told me to meet her on that beach. She wanted it as much as I did.'

'And she wanted her throat cut too?' asked Vlora.

Vasilis replied. 'When I left her, she was fine. We'd made love and she wanted to stay on the beach by herself.'

'Fucking bullshit, Vasilis. You put her through hell and you left her for dead, you lying bastard,' said Dimitris.

Vasilis raged back. 'No. She's the fucking liar. She has got you all fooled, running around reacting to her lies. Where the fuck is she anyway?'

Vlora could take it no longer. She reached into her bag and began to pull out a gun, exposing its grip to everyone. Dimitris grabbed her hand and pushed it back into her bag. 'No Vlora, not here.'

Vasilis reacted by lifting the table and throwing it over the trio, then he made a dash for the exit. His action gave him a head start, as he stormed out of the hotel and down the steps, he ran past Mikalis and Maria. Seconds later, the trio stormed past them, also in hot pursuit.

Jordan was in the process of relating everything to Mikalis, but it all happened too fast to warn him and Maria, he was only left with the option to shout into the phone. 'Get after them.'

Mikalis held the phone to his ear as he and Maria set chase. 'It's time to call this in Jordan. I'm calling the cops now. Try and keep an eye on things from up there. You may have to direct the cops when they get here.'

Vasilis had already entered the myriad of lanes and near vertical steps that covered the cliff rim of Imerovigli with some of the most expensive and luxurious real estate in the Mediterranean. He was pushing past tourists as they meandered casually around the narrow walkways and took photos of the villas and their magnificent infinity pools that overlooked one of the world's greatest natural vistas. The afternoon heat and the challenging layout of pathways were rapidly draining him of his energy. He had to find somewhere to rest and he was running out of ways to go, he had already reached the lowest extent of dwellings that populated the cliff faces. A small white church set in its own courtyard was right in front of him. He looked around to make sure he was alone. Vasilis caught his breath and entered the open courtyard and made his way to the front of the church. There was a space of a couple of metres between the church frontage and a low wall. He gazed over the wall, the church was built out on a crop of black rocks with a vertical drop of more than 50 metres. The rocks then gave way to a long very steep incline that fell all the way to the sea. There was no escape for him that way, he was looking at a total drop of 300 metres or more. Vasilis stepped back and sat against the front wall of the church and tried to control his breathing to remain as quiet as he could.

It was not long before Jordan and Katerina lost their viewing advantage from the bell tower, they lost sight of everyone as they all disappeared down into the steep walkways that ran between the white walls of the tightly packed buildings.

Mikalis called Jordan again and said. 'We've lost them Jordan, can you see anything from where you are?'

'Sorry pal. There are just too many obstacles in the way.' Jordan took one last look from his elevated position. 'Hold on, I have an idea.' At the base of the tower, Jordan saw someone operating a drone. He and Katerina came down from the tower and rushed over to the operator. Jordon asked the owner if he could use his drone. They all gathered around the display as Jordan scanned the area below. He piloted the drone outwards and dropped it down to pick up the buildings at the lowest point. Then he gradually brought it back in to give close up shots of what was down there. Katerina spotted the man sitting at the front of the church and Jordan zoomed in. It was Vasilis. Jordan started elevating the drone to scan the walkways that led to the church and located the trio. They were closing in on their prey. He raised the drone higher and found Mikalis and Maria.

He told Mikalis, 'Keep going until you reach the bottom and can see a white church, you're only a minute or two behind them. Vasilis is hiding at the front of the church. Be careful.'

Katerina told Jordan that she could hear the sound of the police siren getting closer. Jordan handed the controls for the drone back to its owner. 'Thanks mate, when the cops get here, direct them to the church please.' Then he and Katerina set off to catch up with the others.

The trio reached the church and realised that they had arrived at the lowest point. Vlora pushed her way to the front and her brother stopped her. 'No Vlora, I'm going first.'

Mergim entered the courtyard and worked his way around the left hand side of the church towards the front. Vlora and Dimitris followed him. Vasilis heard them and stood up and leaned against the wall. As

Mergim peered around the front of the church, Vasilis grabbed him and swung him around to face the others and moved backwards, towards the low wall and the drop.

Mikalis and Maria arrived. They could see the backs of Dimitris and Vlora but that was all. They worked their way around the right hand side of the church then stopped and listened.

Vasilis was threatening to throw Mergim over the wall and trying to bargain his way out.

Jordan and Katerina reached the church and moved around to join Mikalis and Maria. They huddled together, unable to speak or use their phones. Mikalis mouthed the words, "The police." Jordan pointed down with his finger to indicate that they were on their way.

Vlora drew her gun and pointed it at Vasilis's head.

Vasilis stepped back and pulled Mergim to the edge of the wall, inches away from the drop. He shouted out. 'Put the gun away or he goes over.'

Mikalis was unarmed, all he had was his police badge. He looked at the others and shook his head as if to suggest he could do nothing.

Dimitris said. 'Would you take the life of your own son Vasilis?'

'Nice try Dimitris.'

'Figure it out Vasilis, he is 27 years old.'

'There you go, fucking lying again,' said Vasilis. As he shouted out the words of denial, he turned slightly to push Mergim closer to the drop.

The police had made their way to the roof of an adjacent building. The tourist with the drone had given them a bird's eye view of the stand-off a few minutes earlier to orientate them.

Vlora fired a shot and hit Vasilis in the shoulder. Mergim fell forwards and scrambled to hold onto the wall as he hung over the edge.

Jordan and the others heard another shot, followed by cries from the police for everyone to stand still. Mikalis emerged from the other side of the church, held up his police badge and made eye contact with the policemen on the roof. They acknowledged him and he walked around to survey the scene and take charge, followed by the others.

Vlora and Vasilis were lying on the ground, both wounded. Mergim was hanging off the edge of the wall crying for help and Dimitris was nowhere to be seen. He had made a run for it, when he heard the second shot being fired.

Jordan ran to Mergim to try and help him. Katerina saw Vlora attempting to reach for the gun that lay in front of her. She instinctively ran over and kicked the gun away from Vlora's reach. Katerina bent over to look Vlora in the eyes and smiled when Vlora recognised her. Then she headed over to help Jordan try and rescue Mergim.

Mergim's face lit up when he saw Katerina. Jordan had a grip of him by his shirt and Katerina tried to pull him by his arm but the gravity was winning. Mergim's shirt ripped and he fell away. Jordan hugged Katerina and turned her face away from the edge. By now Vlora was being attended to by the police that had arrived at the scene. Vlora witnessed Katerina's sadness at not being able to save Mergim and nodded to her. It was a sentiment that said. "Thanks for trying."

Dimitris had only made it up three flights of steps before he was apprehended. He was returned to the scene and formally arrested along with Vlora and Vasilis. The wounded pair were air lifted away from the church by a helicopter and taken to hospital and Dimitris was marched back up the stairways and taken to the police station.

✿

CHAPTER TWENTY FOUR

Sunday16th June. Morning

Santorini

Dimitris sat in the same interview room where he had been questioned 28 years ago. The eyes and the look of the old Detective conducting the interview were unmistakable.

Dimitris said. 'You must be getting near your retirement age.'

'Do we know each other?'

'Yes we do. Can you recall an incident 28 years ago? A young Albanian girl, slashed throat....'

The Detective put his hand up to silence Dimitris and paused the tape recorder and asked the accompanying police officer to leave the room. 'Go on. Finish what you were saying.'

Dimitris reminded the Detective of the decision he had made to eliminate the claim of rape and attempted murder of his girlfriend to protect the reputation of the island.

The Detective was visibly uncomfortable, but retained an air of arrogance as he responded. 'That was a long time ago. Things were different then. What makes you think that information will help you now?'

'You're right, times were different then. We all have more rights now and you owe me, you bastard. I am sure you are looking forward to picking up your pension. You wouldn't want me to get in the way of that would you?'

The Detective adopted a more sympathetic tone and said. 'Go on.'

Dimitris continued. 'Look, I am prepared to tell you everything I know, but I need a promise from you that you will do the right thing by Donika this time.'

The Detective gave the promise and listened intently as Dimitris recounted everything that had happened since Donika had revealed her secret on her death bed a few months earlier. Dimitris divulged everything, the abductions, the framing of Vasilis and the accidental death of Emilia. When he finished the Detective said. 'You understand that you have implicated yourself heavily in this?'

'I do, and if that is the price I have to pay, then so be it. All I ever wanted was to bring him to justice,' said Dimitris.

The Detective held out his hand and Dimitris accepted his offer and shook it.

'Rest assured. We have enough leverage to get Vasilis Kostas to confess to the rape and attempted murder. Plus we have DNA now, that always makes our job easier.' As the Detective turned to leave the interview room he said. 'By the way, we recovered Mergim's body from the sea.'

Early evening
Oia, Santorini.

The best point to watch the sunset on Santorini is from the town of Oia, situated on the north west tip of the Island. Every possible viewing point is crammed with people waiting for the colourful spectacle to begin. Mikalis had called in a few favours with his new local police colleagues and managed to secure a front table at a rooftop restaurant to share the experience with Katerina, Maria and Jordan. He was footing the bill as a thank you to his friends in return for the kudos he was now receiving in his role as a valued police officer. They had all spent the rest of Saturday evening at the police station, giving statements. But it was Katerina's evidence that would write the case to prosecute Vlora for her crimes.

The sunset did not disappoint any of the thousands of tourists that lined the streets and rooftops to bask in the unique orange glow that surrounded them and decorated the buildings.

Mikalis deliberately waited until the end of the evening to tell the story of why and how the Vokshi's and their friend Dimitris had waged their vengeance on Vasilis Kostas across these islands over the past few weeks. It changed the mood of the evening dramatically and seemed to have a profound effect on Katerina. Maria walked around the table to kneel next to her. 'Are you okay?'

'It's terrible Maria. They've lost everything. And poor Donika, it's so sad?'

Maria hugged her friend and they shed tears together.

Monday 17th June, Morning

Santorini

Dimitris heard the cell door open and watched as the Detective walked in and came over to sit alongside him.

'I have some news for you and I am not sure how to tell you.'

Dimitris shrugged his shoulders and replied. 'Then just say it.'

'Well first of all, we got a full confession from Vasilis. He is going down for the rape and attempted murder of Donika.'

Dimitris could not contain his joy at hearing that news. He was smiling from ear to ear until he looked at the Detective and his expression. 'What's wrong?'

'Vasilis assumed that we had DNA proof that Mergim was his son. We didn't tell him any different of course.'

'So, you got him anyway.'

The Detective looked Dimitris in the eyes. 'Mergim's DNA is a match for yours Dimitris. He was your son.'

The words hit him like a freight train. How could that be? Mergim was always the child of Vasilis Kostas. It's what Donika had always believed, and it is what she had told him on her death bed. He closed his eyes and the memory came back to him. The night in Aegina, when she had come to his room. They had cried in each other's arms and made love, only once and he was so careful.

The Detective touched Dimitris on his shoulder and said. 'I am sorry. I felt you had to know.' As he walked to the cell door he turned and said. 'I am the only one that has seen that report. There is no need to share that with anyone. I owe you that, Dimitris.'

Dimitris quietly uttered the words. 'Thank you.'

—

Wednesday 19th June, Afternoon
Santorini Airport

Mikalis and Katerina met Jordan and Maria in the coffee shop outside the small but extremely busy airport. Jordan had persuaded Maria to come to England with him, it would give them a chance to get to know each other in a fresh environment, away from the madness of the last few weeks. He told her she would love Canterbury, and as a historian, there would be plenty for her to investigate.

Mikalis and Katerina only had a few minutes to bid their friends farewell or kalo taxidi as they say it in Greek. They all sat and chatted for a while, squeezing the most of their last few moments together.

Jordan asked Mikalis what his plans were. He told them that he had applied for a transfer to Santorini and that it had been approved.

When Maria asked Katerina what her plans were, she said. 'I came to these islands to follow my dream and that is what I am going to do. Perhaps I can combine some of my dreams with the ones that Donika never got to finish.'

—

As the aircraft set its course it banked right. The angle gave Maria and Jordan a clear view of the Santorini

Caldera. Jordan leaned over and hugged Maria as they looked down at the massive cliffs. They could see that two large ferries were offloading hundreds of passengers at the port. The visitors were coming to enjoy the natural beauty of the Cyclades islands, the Greek Philoxenia, and to escape the stresses and complexities of their lives. Some of them had read about the incident that had occurred recently on the Caldera but they were assured by the reports that it was an isolated domestic incident and that they had nothing to fear.

As the plane left Santorini behind, Maria pointed out the islands of Ios, Koufonisia, Irakleia, Naxos, Paros and Antiparos. Jordan knew they would return together to visit them one day.

THE END

Glossary of Greek words
used in this book

Efharisto – Thank you

Chora – The main town of an island

Platia – The town square

Yasas – A greeting used for both "hello" and "goodbye"

Gyros – Meet cooked on a vertical rotisserie

Malaka – A derogatory term translating as "jerk".

Kalimera – A greeting used in the morning

Kalispera – A greeting used in the later part of the day

Philoxenia – A term used to describe warmth and hospitality shown to strangers

Kato – Below or lower

Ano – Upper or above

Oriste – Go ahead or you have my attention. Often used when accepting a phone call

Filakia – Lots of kisses

Ela – Come! But sometimes used as an expression of surprise

Ti kanis – How are you?

Poly kala – Very good

Yamas – Cheers or a toast for health

Spanakopita – A traditional Greek pie made with
spinach, feta cheese and filo pastry

Agia – Saint

Bougatsa – A Greek breakfast pasty, sweet or salty,
made with a variety of fillings
Koukla – Dolly, used as a term of endearment
Kalo taxidi – Travel well

www.ingramcontent.com/pod-product-compliance
Lightning Source LLC
Chambersburg PA
CBHW020100180626
46812CB00006B/2404